TRACKTOWN
SUMMER

TRACKTOWN SUMMER

ELIZABETH HOLMES

DUTTON CHILDREN'S BOOKS

DUTTON CHILDREN'S BOOKS
A division of Penguin Young Readers Group

Published by the Penguin Group
Penguin Group (USA) Inc., 375 Hudson Street, New York, New York 10014, U.S.A.
Penguin Group (Canada), 90 Eglinton Avenue East, Suite 700, Toronto, Ontario M4P 2Y3,
Canada (a division of Pearson Penguin Canada Inc.) ▪ Penguin Books Ltd, 80 Strand, London
WC2R 0RL, England ▪ Penguin Ireland, 25 St Stephen's Green, Dublin 2, Ireland (a division
of Penguin Books Ltd) ▪ Penguin Group (Australia), 250 Camberwell Road, Camberwell,
Victoria 3124, Australia (a division of Pearson Australia Group Pty Ltd) ▪ Penguin Books India
Pvt Ltd, 11 Community Centre, Panchsheel Park, New Delhi - 110 017, India ▪ Penguin Group
(NZ), 67 Apollo Drive, Rosedale, North Shore 0632, New Zealand (a division of Pearson New
Zealand Ltd.) ▪ Penguin Books (South Africa) (Pty) Ltd, 24 Sturdee Avenue, Rosebank, Johan-
nesburg 2196, South Africa ▪ Penguin Books Ltd, Registered Offices: 80 Strand, London
WC2R 0RL, England

This book is a work of fiction. Names, characters, places, and incidents are either the product of
the author's imagination or are used fictitiously, and any resemblance to actual persons, living or
dead, business establishments, events, or locales is entirely coincidental.

The publisher does not have any control over and does not assume any responsibility for
author or third-party websites or their content.

Library of Congress Cataloging-in-Publication Data

Holmes, Elizabeth Ann, date.
Tracktown summer / Elizabeth Holmes.—1st ed.   p. cm.
Summary: Spending the summer with his father at a run-down house between a railroad track
and a polluted section of a lake, twelve-year-old Jake gets involved with a fourteen-year-old
neighbor who is hiding a secret within his home.
ISBN 978-0-525-47946-8
[1. Fathers and sons—Fiction. 2. Secrets—Fiction. 3. Lakes—Fiction.
4. Family problems—Fiction. 5. Mental illness—Fiction.] I. Title.
PZ7.H7355Trc 2009   [Fic]—dc22   2008034223

Published in the United States by Dutton Children's Books,
a division of Penguin Young Readers Group
345 Hudson Street, New York, New York 10014
www.penguin.com/youngreaders

DESIGNED BY ABBY KUPERSTOCK

Printed in USA ▪ First Edition
1 3 5 7 9 10 8 6 4 2

For Paul, Liam, and Austin

TRACKTOWN
SUMMER

CHAPTER 1

It's somewhere along here," Jake's mother said, slowing the car.

For miles the road had been high and level, passing through open farm country, everything spacious and wide. But just now, just before his mother spoke, the road had curved broadly to the left, and for the first time they glimpsed the lake, long and narrow, over to their right. Then the road began to descend, and wooded slopes closed around them, the lake flashing erratically through the trees.

There were more houses now. The ones on the left had tall vertical faces, and their back ends were buried in the hill; some of them looked as though they were about to slide into the road. The houses on the right, next to the lake, were invisible, except for a few roofs and chimneys, because the ground dropped off so steeply.

The June sun was glinting off the hood of the old blue Toyota, and off the oncoming cars and the mailboxes and the glittery speckles in the asphalt road and driveways. "Watch the numbers on the mailboxes," Jake's mother ordered. "It's twenty-three thirty-two."

Jake was irritated. "Like you haven't told me ten times already." Okay, maybe not ten times, but she *had* told him, and only about five minutes ago. He wasn't a little kid who had to be told everything over and over; he was twelve years old. And he didn't like her bossy tone. She sounded tense, and he felt sort of like that himself.

He expected her to tell him to stop being mouthy, but, as he saw out of the corner of his eye, she only clamped her lips together and peered anxiously from the roadside to the rearview mirror and back again.

"Forty-seven eighteen," Jake read off a low sign at the end of a driveway.

"Oh, so we're not that close." The Toyota accelerated a little.

Glancing back, Jake saw four or five cars close behind them and felt as if the cars were pushing them down the hill, hurrying them on to this place they'd never seen. The twitchy tightness in his stomach twitched again.

A few minutes later the descent became less steep, and the land on both sides opened up a little. "Twenty-three sixty!" Jake said, more nervously than he'd meant to. The next time he kept his voice offhand. "Twenty-three forty-eight."

His mother signaled right and pulled way over, slowing to a crawl to let the cars behind them pass. In a moment, signal tinkling, she turned into a bumpy little road that quickly aligned itself parallel to the main road, and there she stopped the car.

There were maybe six or eight small houses along this side road, and for a minute Jake didn't know which was the right one. "Where is it?" he asked, and his mother pointed mutely at a dingy white house with pink trim. Now he saw the house number, black metal digits tacked vertically on the post beside the front steps. She hadn't pulled the car up close to the house, as she could have, Jake noticed. She'd stopped a little way before it, as though to look things over, or to put off actually getting there for a few more moments.

He didn't ask her about this, and neither of them made a move to get out of the car.

Jake felt a sinking inside as he took it all in. There was the main road, and then the little road close alongside it, and then the houses along one side of the road only, and beyond the houses was the lake, huge and sparkling in the sun. But there was nothing sparkling about the houses. They looked cramped and old and in need of paint. They were so close together they didn't have yards, just dirt patches a few feet wide in between them. Most of the cars around them looked even more rusty and dented than Mom's old Toyota.

He hadn't pictured spending the summer in a place like this. He'd pictured something more like the lake house his friend Stephen had. Stephen's family had taken him along for weekends there. The house was a log cabin, but everything was new and modern inside, and it was surrounded by woods; you could barely see the neighboring houses. There was a path down to the dock, where a sleek speedboat was waiting.

He didn't think any speedboat would be waiting for him here.

The pink-trimmed house was probably the shabbiest one on the street. He noticed now that the bottom step was half broken, and a short board had been propped up against it like a warning. He could see a long crack in one of the first-floor windows.

Inside the silent car it was getting hot. As if his mother had the same thought, she put a hand on her door handle. "This is it, kiddo," she said, trying to smile.

"Yeah," he said, and they both got out. At the sound of their doors shutting a curtain moved behind the cracked window, and Jake's mother hurried to open the trunk, but Jake stood staring at the house. Behind him he heard his mother taking things out of the trunk and slamming it shut again.

A man appeared on the front steps and waved to them, coming quickly down the steps.

"Jake!" his mother said urgently, and as he turned toward her she hugged him hard. "I'll call you. I love you so much."

"You're leaving now?" he said, bewildered.

"I just have to," she said, the keys shaking in her hand. "Go on now."

She got in the car and the motor roared. While Jake watched, his mother backed the car away, then wrenched it toward the main road. The car paused at the lip of the road and then pulled out, and Jake turned toward his father.

He was enveloped in a huge hug, and he found himself grinning into his father's shirt even as his insides ached from his mother's sudden leaving. He'd thought she'd stay a little while, not run off like that. He'd imagined his parents drinking coffee together, hanging around together with him, maybe joking around like they used to, before she finally had to get back in her car.

But it was so good to have Dad hugging him. Dad's hugs were so different from Mom's. They were really hard and almost hurt, squishing Jake's ear against a button or squeezing half his breath out, but they were great too. They made him feel like he and Dad were alike, like they were both men, like he was Dad's and Dad was his in a way that was not a mother's way.

Dad was knuckling his shoulder and saying he was wicked glad to see Jake after so long, and they were going to have so much fun together.

When had his father started saying things like "wicked"? Jake didn't ask.

His father released him from the ferocious hug and studied Jake for a moment at arm's length, with his hands on Jake's shoulders. "You're gaining on me," he said.

It was true, Jake could see that. He'd been growing a lot lately; weeks ago, before it got warm enough to wear shorts every day, he'd noticed that his best jeans were too short all of a sudden. His dad wasn't tall, just medium height, stocky and solidly built, and Jake wondered if someday he would actually be taller than Dad.

His father had changed some too, Jake thought. His hair—light brown, with a touch of gray—was a little longer than it used to be, and there was something silky about the gray buttoned shirt he wore—much classier than the T-shirts he used to wear in the summers.

His father's blue eyes shifted from Jake to the road behind him, and the crinkles around them deepened. "Your mother didn't waste any time, did she?"

"She just dropped me and ran." He kept his voice neutral.

His father shrugged. "Well, let's grab your things and I'll show you the place, such as it is."

His father took the big duffel bag, Jake took the backpack, and they headed up the dusty road toward the white-and-pink house. A grubby little girl with blond hair watched them from the porch of the house next door. Cars whizzed past on the highway, but the side road was empty and quiet.

Jake followed his father up the steps, skipping the broken one. The door had a screen like Swiss cheese, and beyond it the air was dim and cool. Jake found himself in a small living room with a black woodstove, a greenish plaid couch, and one lumpy-looking brown armchair.

"I'll give you the grand tour," his father said. It didn't take long. Downstairs was only the living room, the kitchen (which had a little booth—a table and two high-backed benches—in the corner), and the mudroom in the back. Jake stared through the back door at the lake, just beyond the yard and the dock built of gray, weathered boards. The dock was empty. A couple of sailboats were coasting along, far out on the shimmery lake.

They carried the bags upstairs, where there was a bathroom at the top of the stairs and a bedroom to each side. "Here's your castle," Dad said, pointing to the room on the right. It had a bed, a desk with a folding chair, and an orange beanbag chair. One window faced the road; the other faced the house next door, which was only ten or twelve feet away. When Jake looked out, the same little girl was holding onto the porch railing and staring up at him, as if she'd been expecting him to appear right there. She squinted up at him curiously, and he pulled back.

"What's all this stuff?" he asked. The desk was covered with books and papers, and four or five cardboard boxes were piled next to it.

"Work, my friend, work! You don't think I'm on vacation all summer, do you?" His father started gathering up some of the papers. "Don't worry, I'll move it. This room will be all yours."

"You're a teacher," Jake protested. "You're not supposed to work in the summer."

"I *used* to be a teacher," his father said. "Now I'm a professor, and I have to get prepared to teach two new courses in the fall. Also, if I want to keep this job and get tenure some-day, I'd better write a book."

"What's tenure?" Immediately, Jake wished he hadn't asked. He always wanted to know what words meant, but just now he didn't want to know more about professors and colleges and all that. Being a professor was what had taken his father away.

"It means your job is permanent," his father answered, making a neat stack of the books on the desk. "You can say exactly what you think, and even the president of the college can't fire you for saying it. You can't get fired unless you do something really terrible. And it means you get more money and more respect than the people who don't have tenure."

"Oh." Again Jake felt a slow sinking inside. He wasn't really listening to his father's words; he was listening to his voice, his tone. And what he heard was that his father really cared about this stuff, about being a professor. He still cared about it now that he had the job, after all those years when he'd taught high school history all day and worked on his PhD at night and during the summers, and there wasn't much time left for his son.

And then, last summer, he'd been hired by a small college almost five hundred miles away, and he had moved. He'd driven away in the station wagon, with a rented trailer hitched behind it, and Jake had stood on the front porch and watched until his father turned the corner at the end of the block. As the station wagon turned, the side windows glared blankly in the sun, and Jake couldn't see anyone inside to wave to, and he didn't wave.

His father made spaghetti and salad for dinner, and they ate sitting across from each other in the booth in the kitchen.

"This is like the Pine Tree Diner," Jake said, sliding to the middle of the green bench. "The plates too—they're just like the ones at the diner." Thick and heavy, the plates had once been white but were now grayish in the center from the scratches of countless knives and forks.

His father smiled. "I'll take you to a good diner here sometime. A lot better than the old Pine Tree." He broke off a piece of garlic bread from a foil-wrapped loaf. "Hey, how's the spaghetti?"

"Good." Jake was trying to twirl the spaghetti carefully on his fork, the way his father had always told him to, instead of stuffing in a forkful and letting strings of pasta hang out of his mouth. At home he'd never paid much attention to his parents' comments about table manners, but now, in front of his father after so long, he found himself wanting to look mature.

Anyway, Dad didn't seem to notice, even when Jake messed up and had to quickly wipe off a spaghetti-sauce beard with his napkin.

"How'd your baseball season end up?" his father asked.

Jake looked up from his pasta. "I told you, don't you remember? Thirteen and eleven. I told you on the phone last time."

"You did? Well, I'm getting old—the memory goes, you know, when you get to be an old geezer." His father grinned in an apologetic way, but Jake felt anger souring his stomach.

"Yeah, right." He chewed on some garlic bread in silence.

"Well," his father hesitated, then said, too heartily, "your pitching was getting better, I remember that."

"Oh sure," Jake said sarcastically. "I probably have the all-time record for walks." This wasn't quite fair, a voice was saying in the back of his mind; his pitching really had improved, and he'd told his father that on the phone. But still, the second half of the season had been hard, after their best pitcher had managed to fall out of a tree and break his arm. Jake had had to do a lot of the pitching after that, and he was pretty bad. He'd allowed a lot of hits, and thrown a lot of balls that went nowhere near the plate, and felt his face redden and his stomach clench, with everybody's eyes on him.

It would have meant so much to have Dad there, cheering him on at the games, giving him tips, practicing with him in the backyard. But Dad was five hundred miles away. He'd seen exactly two of Jake's games, and in the first one Jake didn't pitch at all, just played second base. The two games were on weekends when his father came back to visit, which he did about once a month. He never let Jake come to visit him. He said his apartment near the college was too small, and there was nothing to do there.

His father sighed and laid his fork on his plate. "Well, let's clear up, if you're done." He slid out of the booth, taking his plate and the salad bowl over to the counter. Jake followed, putting his own plate in the sink. He slid his hands into the pockets of his jean shorts and turned toward the living room. Maybe he'd watch some TV.

"Hang on, Jake, we've got cleanup to do," his father said. "No dishwasher here."

Reluctantly Jake turned back. He made his voice slow. "What am I supposed to do?"

"Clear the table and put things in the fridge while I wash the dishes. We can switch next time."

Silently Jake did as his father asked. He was just glad he didn't have to wash the gross plates with tomato sauce all over them. Maybe tomorrow he could talk Dad into washing the dishes every night.

He put the milk and grated cheese in the refrigerator, listening to the clatter of dishes in the sink and his father quietly whistling "Sweet Georgia Brown" as he washed. It was just the way Dad used to whistle at home when he loaded the dishwasher, which was always his job, because Mom always cooked dinner. Dad always whistled while he did it, and he never whistled any other time.

With a glance back to make sure the table was clear, Jake

headed into the living room, going straight for the TV. It looked old, and it was a lot smaller than the one he and Mom had at home. In fact, he didn't know anybody who had a TV that small. He pushed the power button, then looked around for the remote while the set crackled on.

He found the remote on the lower shelf of the coffee table, stretched out on the couch, and began surfing for something to watch.

His father appeared in the kitchen doorway, drying his hands on a ragged dish towel. "The Yankees game starts at eight—want to watch?"

"Sure." Jake brightened; he'd always loved watching games with his father. "This is a tiny TV, though. I've never even seen one this small."

"Yeah. Sam told me when he rented me this place that we could watch the games, but the players would all be midgets."

His father disappeared long enough to put the towel away, and Jake's eyes went back to the screen. "Who is this Sam guy, anyway?" he asked as he flipped past ads for coffee, antacids, cars, detergent.

"A colleague of mine."

"What the heck is a colleague?" Jake asked, even though he sort of knew.

"Someone I work with. Another professor at the college. He grew up here, and he usually spends the summers here.

But his wife is seriously ill, so he couldn't come this summer. He's renting it to me at a very reasonable rate."

His father leaned in the doorway, folding his arms. "I thought it would be a nice place for you and me to spend some time together." He looked intently into Jake's eyes, which shifted away before Jake could stop them.

And then his eyes went wide. For a few seconds he'd been hearing a low and distant rumble, hardly different from the normal sounds of the highway. But now it was rapidly growing louder and louder, and the floor under his feet was trembling, and then the whole house was shaking. He jumped to his feet.

"What the hell is that?" he shouted over the noise. His heart was hammering.

His father grinned, standing there with his feet apart, as though balancing himself on the swaying deck of a ship. Before he could answer the question, or tell Jake not to say "hell," the air was torn by the unmistakable blast of a train whistle. Mouth open, Jake ran to the front door just in time to see an enormous black engine rush into view. There was a train track maybe twenty-five feet away, running between the little road and the highway.

He stood and stared, enveloped in sound, as car after car rumbled and clattered and squealed past him. Most were boxcars, gray or black or rusty red, with a few mysterious words or numbers stenciled on them with white paint, giving no clue to their contents. From the engine a long double blast floated back, short then long, somehow both majestic and threatening.

Jake opened the door and stepped out onto the little front porch, then went down the steps and stood in the road, gazing at the train. He'd never been this close to a moving train, at least not without being sealed inside a car. It was fascinating and powerful and a little scary. He wished he was driving that massive engine.

He didn't know how many cars had passed—it must have been at least fifty—when the last one clattered off down the track, leaving a curious emptiness. Around the tracks a scattering of tall weeds swayed in a slight breeze. Along the highway, no longer blocked from view, a couple of cars forged steadily uphill and a pickup truck was coasting down, just as though nothing had happened.

Of course, nothing *had* happened. It was just a train passing, exactly the way trains must pass by here every single day . . . He turned back to the house, where his father was sitting on the top step. "Hey, Dad."

"Yes?"

"How many times a day does that thing go by?"

"You mean *those things*. It's not the same train every time."

"*Duhhh*," said Jake, flapping his arms in exasperation. His father always had to be so precise. "Okay, so how many times a day does *a train*, some train or other, pass by this house?"

"Four." His father sat with his hands on his knees, looking

down on Jake. "Nine-thirty in the morning going north, two in the afternoon going south, seven in the evening north-bound. And then another southbound at four A.M."

"Four A.M.? Holy samoly—you mean that thing wakes you up every night at four A.M.?"

"It does indeed. If you ask some of the people who've lived here for ten or twenty years, they claim they can sleep right through it. I don't know if I believe that, though."

"Weird," said Jake. "Maybe they use earplugs."

His father shook his head. "Earplugs don't help that much. The noise is just too loud, and anyway, your bed shakes. I don't bother with the plugs anymore, but you can try them if you want to."

His father stood up. "Well, the show's over. Why don't we go upstairs and get you settled in before time for the game?"

CHAPTER

2

IIII IIIII

Jake was deep in a dream that somehow involved his sixth-grade math teacher, a go-cart race, and a plate of French toast when his mother started shaking him to wake him up for school. " 'S too early," he mumbled, pulling the cotton blanket up around his ears. But she kept after him, and she was making a ridiculous amount of noise, like she was moving the furniture in his bedroom or something. Why was she doing that so early in the morning? Why couldn't she let him sleep?

But she just made more and more noise, and finally his eyes popped open and he saw the desk and the beanbag chair in the yellowish glow that poured in his window from a streetlight. His bed was shaking like there was a sputtering motor inside it, and the tremendous screeching clatter of the train was ricocheting all around the room.

Jake's heart was beating fast, and he scrunched up in the bed and squeezed his hands together. It's just the train, it's just the train, he told himself. He wanted to go to his father, but at the same time he didn't want to get out of bed. It was almost as if he couldn't, as if the noise was a whirling wind that kept him pinned to the mattress.

At last the noise began to move off, the pressure of it eased, and the rattle was no bigger than the sound of someone rummaging through cutlery in a kitchen drawer. When the whistle blast came, short then long, it was distant enough to drift back to him, smoky and musical.

Jake felt his breathing and his heartbeat return to normal, but now he was wide awake. What was all that about go-carts? A race, and Mrs. Marshall, the math teacher, fired the starter's pistol. He grinned to himself. The idea of Mrs. Marshall—who had curly gray hair and wore suits to work—firing a starter's pistol for a go-cart race was pretty funny, although in the dream it had seemed perfectly normal.

His friend Stephen had been in the race too. Stephen's dad made the world's best French toast; maybe that explained the blue plate piled high with thick slices of it, dripping with maple syrup. In the dream he'd stopped watching the race and moved toward the French toast, which was somehow nearby, on Stephen's kitchen table.

Jake sighed. The dream had ended before he could find out whether he'd get the French toast or not. Ended with his mother shaking him, which of course was really the train shaking the whole house.

He heard footsteps, and his father stood in the doorway, running a hand through his tousled hair and yawning.

Jake sat up. "Hi, Dad."

"Shocking, isn't it?" his father said. "The first time you get woken up by it."

"It messed up a good dream," Jake said, not wanting to admit how much it had scared him.

"Well, now you can get back to sleep. Maybe the dream will come back."

His father turned to go, and quickly Jake said, "But I'm wide-awake."

"So am I. I'm going down to make a cup of coffee."

"I'm coming too." Jake jumped out of bed and padded down the stairs after his father, the wood cool and dusty under his bare feet.

His father turned on a small bright light over the stove, put water in the kettle, and twisted a knob, making the gas flare wide and yellow, then swiftly resolve itself into a ring of little blue flames.

While his father was busy with the filter and cup and coffee can, Jake prowled around the shadowy kitchen, opening cupboards, looking in drawers.

"What are you looking for?" his father asked.

"Nothing. Just looking." It was exciting, being up at this hour, with his father, in this strange little house. He went into the mudroom behind the kitchen and looked out the window at the lake, silvery with moonlight. He came back into the kitchen, beating a quick rhythm on the table with his palms. He was brimming with something, only he didn't know what it was.

From the table he moved on to tattooing the counter, the sink, the door frame.

"Must you do that?" his father growled. He put the coffee can back in a cupboard, then turned to look at Jake, who gave the door frame a few parting taps before saying, "Sorry. Hey, can I have some coffee too?"

"No," said his father drily. "No, you may not."

"Well, golly gee gosh darn dangit," said Jake, who had known perfectly well that he wasn't going to be allowed to drink coffee.

"When you wake up, you really wake up, don't you, Jake?" sighed his father. "You always did."

"What are we going to do now?" Jake asked.

The kettle began to whistle faintly, and his father turned off the gas and poured water into the filter. "*I*," he finally answered, "am going upstairs to work for a while, just as I always do after the train wakes me up. *You* are going back to bed."

"I'm too wide-awake."

"Read a book, then." His father poured more water into the filter.

"Make me some French toast?" He gave his father his most winning smile.

"No," said his father. "I'm going up to work. You can make your own, I guess." He put the dripping filter into the sink and picked up his mug.

"I don't know how."

"Of course you do. Mix up some egg and milk, dip the bread in it, and fry it in the pan." He turned toward the stairs, then turned back, his eyes narrowed a little. "Are you allowed to use the stove at home?"

"Like, *duhhh*." He'd been making himself macaroni and cheese long before Dad left.

"I take that to mean yes."

Grumpily, Jake scuffed one foot against the floor, back and forth, then looked up again. "Will you make it for me? Please?"

His father shook his head. "Sorry, Jake. I really need to stick to my routine, or I won't get anything done. You'll be fine. Get something to eat, and then you'll get back to sleep in no time." He walked out of the kitchen, and Jake followed a few steps to watch from the bottom as his father went up the stairs. His white T-shirt showed up in the dim light from upstairs, but his dark boxers and his legs were hardly visible at all.

Jake went back in the kitchen and kicked the stove.

He stood there for a minute, staring at the stove without seeing it, his foot throbbing. Then he turned out the light and went upstairs. He barely glanced to the left, where his father's door was closed, with a thin bar of light showing under it. In his own room he turned on the desk lamp and got a book out of his backpack. Then he punched the beanbag chair into shape, sat down, jammed the open book against his knees, and forced his eyes to move across the words.

■ ■ ■

When Jake woke up it was late, past nine o'clock. He got up and pulled on shorts, then went out to the stair landing. His father's door was open now, and Jake peered in. Dad was snoring softly in the bed. Light filtered through the curtains covering the two windows that faced out over the lake. On the desk the laptop's screen saver was endlessly painting mesmerizing swirls of color.

For a minute Jake's eyes followed the irresistible motion of the changing colors, and then he turned and went downstairs, through the kitchen and the mudroom, and out the back door.

The sky was bright but hazy, the air warm and humid. Jake went down the rough wooden steps to the yard, hardly bigger than a room, scruffy with patches of dirt and grass and stones.

The air smelled damp and slightly fishy. Jake walked right into the lake, just up to his ankles in the cold water, his feet slipping a little on the rounded stones. He bent over and picked up some flat ones, then skipped them one by one out across the broad surface of the lake. Most of them made no more than three or four hops before sinking. Jake hoped he'd get better at this, spending a whole summer beside a lake. Stephen claimed that he'd once made a rock skip eleven times.

Jake splashed his way over to the dock and walked out to

the very end. The lake was huge, blue-gray, and glittery on the tips of the little wavelets kicked up by the light wind. On the far side he could see some large houses; to the left, maybe a half mile off, was a park at one end of the lake. To the right, the far end was lost in the distance.

Few boats were out, and Jake remembered that it was Monday—the first Monday without school in ages. He grinned at the thought. He was free, and standing alone on the edge of a big lake first thing in the morning was as good a way as any to really *feel* free.

Of course, he couldn't feel entirely alone. The houses were so close together—a row of seven along the little road, marked off at one end, the end toward the park, by a narrow, rocky area with no room for houses. His dad's house—Sam's house—was the second from that end.

He couldn't see what marked off the other end, but these seven houses were clearly their own little neighborhood. Each had its own dock, though some of them looked half rotten, and at three of them, small boats were tied up, open boats with oars and outboard motors, probably used for fishing. A fourth dock had a boat also, this one a bigger, fancier motorboat with water skis propped up in the back.

No one else in the neighborhood seemed to be out, but Jake's sense of freedom faded into a slightly uneasy curiosity as he looked back from the end of the dock to the houses with their blank windows. He wondered if anyone was watching him, maybe wondering who the new kid was. He wondered where the grubby little blond girl was, and whether she had older brothers.

When the train came blasting through, he watched from the dock. It wasn't quite so overwhelming from here, farther away and out in the open. The sound, instead of echoing around a room, had the whole atmosphere, the vast empty air over the lake, to expand in.

The passing boxcars gave a couple of particularly harsh squeals of protesting metal. Glancing back at the lake, Jake saw that a mother duck had come up alongside the dock next door, six fluffy babies trailing her as neatly as if tied on a string. They didn't seem the least bit alarmed by the train.

He waited till the train was gone, then headed inside in search of breakfast.

Later that morning Jake wandered down the train tracks, looking curiously at the houses. He was half hoping to meet other kids, but he was nervous too. His father—who had had breakfast with him and then had gone back to work—had said he'd seen several kids around, and at least a couple of them looked to be about Jake's age. But his father hadn't met any of them and didn't know which houses they lived in.

Jake walked on one of the rails, putting one sneaker right in front of the other on the smooth metal. Between houses he glimpsed a woman hanging laundry on a line in a backyard. An old man was sitting in a lawn chair on the porch at the third house he passed, doing nothing at all, as far as Jake could see. Maybe just soaking up the sun, which was now very high but still shone on the old man's bare, skinny legs. The day was getting hot.

At the very last house in the row, no one was in sight, but there was one thing that caught Jake's eye—a basketball hoop, right out front on the street.

He looked carefully at the house. Both the screen door and the main door behind it were closed. Walking farther down the tracks, he got a better look into the backyard, but no one was there either.

He'd thought his dad's house was the shabbiest one in the row, but this one was worse. It was gray with blue trim, and a lot of the paint was peeling off. But what really made it look shabby was all the stuff lying around. There was a ratty old armchair on the porch—the kind of chair that belongs inside a house, not outside. On the ground near the front steps lay a weird assortment of things—a couple of squirt guns, a rusty garden hoe, a bicycle tire, a cardboard box, a plastic baseball bat.

There was also a basketball—a good one, full-size and new looking. It was just lying there next to the bottom step, and Jake's fingers itched to pick it up. He imagined a quick dribble, dodge, fake, a slam dunk. He could almost feel the ball singing off his hands and swishing through the net.

But it wasn't his ball. He could go over and knock on the door, introduce himself, see if there was a kid there who wanted to play some hoops with him. That was probably what Dad would tell him to do. But that would be embarrassing. No, he couldn't do that.

He walked back and forth, eyes down so he could make each step land on a railroad tie. Then he stopped and looked at the house again. He was so bored. Even playing basketball by himself would be better than just hanging around like this. Maybe no one was home, and he could just play a little and they'd never know.

Maybe someone *was* home, a grown-up who'd come out and yell at him.

He stared a moment longer, then said to himself, What the heck.

Very casually he strolled across the road and picked up the ball. He didn't look at the house. He spun the ball between his hands, then moved closer to the basket and took a shot. It ricocheted off the backboard and bounced once before he caught it. Another shot—*swish*. He dribbled back, then forward for a layup. Now he was in a rhythm, in constant motion, dribbling, shooting, rebounding. He was Paul Pierce, he was Kevin Garnett, turning, weaving, sending the ball through his legs, behind his back, faking out every defender, driving hard for the layup—

Bang. The unmistakable sound of a door slamming—the screen door of this house. Jake's stomach hit the ground before the ball did. He turned slowly toward the door, while the ball scuttered into a bush.

Standing on the top step was a boy slightly bigger than

Jake, a wiry boy with extremely short brown hair, a boy in a red Rockets jersey and black shorts and high-top basketball shoes. The boy didn't look angry and he didn't look friendly. He just stared at Jake, a sizing-up stare. Then he sauntered down the steps and over to the ball, which he pulled out from underneath the bush.

He tossed the ball to Jake, who held it uncertainly for a moment, then took a shot. The other boy seized the rebound, and the ball sailed over Jake's head and dropped cleanly through the net.

They played one-on-one for an hour with hardly a word. The other boy was taller and faster, but Jake was good enough to stay in the game, keep him on his toes. When they finally stopped, hot and panting, Jake flopped down in the shade at the side of the house.

"Want some water?" the other boy said.

"Sure." Jake got up to follow him into the house, but the boy said, "I'll bring some out," and in a second he was up the steps and the screen door had closed behind him. The odd thing was that, as Jake watched, the main door too swung shut. It was as if the other boy wanted to make sure that Jake didn't follow him, or that he couldn't see inside.

The boy came back with two huge plastic cups filled with ice and water. Jake slurped his down gratefully. Both of them leaned against the house in the narrow strip of shade.

"You on a team at school?" the boy asked.

"No. We don't have a real team for sixth grade, just intramurals," Jake admitted, feeling small. This boy was obviously older. "I'll be in seventh next year. Think I'll go out for the team then," he added casually.

"So, what are you, like, twelve?"

"Yeah. How old are you?"

"Fourteen."

"Oh." Jake took another gulp of water. "My name's Jake."

"Jake what?"

"Berry."

"Berry? Like strawberry?" The boy said this without the least flicker of a smile on his thin face. It might have been a jab, as if he thought the name was dumb, or it might have been a simple question.

"No, like blueberry," Jake retorted. "What's your name?"

"Adrian Greene."

"Like green beans?"

This time Adrian grinned. "With an *e* on the end."

They drank their water for a few minutes without talking. The neighborhood was quiet, except for the almost constant dull roaring of cars and trucks on the highway, and the occasional bee buzzing past, and the rattle of ice in their cups.

"Did you just move here or something?" Adrian said finally.

"I'm just here for the summer. I really live in Syracuse. Well, I live in Wendell—it's right outside Syracuse. My dad is renting a house down there." He pointed down the street.

Adrian squinted. "Oh, Sam Weesner's house."

"Yeah. Are there any other guys around? Like our age, sort of?"

"Nope. Closest one is Peter. In that house where the old man always sits on the porch? But he's only in fourth grade, or maybe fifth." Adrian spat some water on a sunny patch of bare ground, which soaked it up instantly. "Right next to your place there's a bunch of girls."

"You mean that little blond girl, like, about three years old?"

"Yeah, Maddy. She's got two big sisters. The one, Allie, she's in my class, she's pretty cool. Then there's the oldest one, Wendy—all she does is work at the Big Top Market and make out with her boyfriend in his car every night. Right over there." He pointed to the dead end of the street, just beyond his house, where a rocky slope blocked any view of whatever lay beyond it. "They're so dumb, they think nobody knows they're there. Sometimes if my window's open I can *hear* them." He rolled his eyes.

"Oooooh," Jake said, contorting his whole body in shudders and grimaces.

"So that's it," Adrian said. "That's Tracktown."

"Tracktown? Is that what you call this place?"

"That's what everybody calls it. Except the jerks that call it Trashtown."

"Why are they so snotty? It's cool to live right beside a lake," Jake said.

"Yeah, it's cool if you live in the *fancy* houses." Adrian gestured again toward the end of the street. "There aren't any more houses for about a mile, because it's too steep. And then the tracks and the highway get farther away from the lake, and there are a lot of rich people's houses. Huge places with thirty-foot sailboats, and BMWs and Mercedes."

Adrian kicked a rock out into the street, and then another one. "Tracktown is the only place where the trains run right by your front door."

3

That afternoon Jake's father said they could go swimming at Clipper's Point, a few miles up the lake. "Why not right here?" Jake said, looking out the window at the gray dock. They were standing in his father's room, where his father was shutting down the laptop and putting away some papers.

His father shook his head. "I don't want you swimming here. This whole end of the lake is shallow and stagnant and polluted."

"It looks clean," Jake said, surprised.

"Well, it's not. The discharge from the sewage treatment plant is about a quarter-mile down that way." He pointed to a spot not far from the park. "And there are pipes that bring in the run-off from the city streets."

"Gross," Jake said. He looked glumly out at the vast green surface. He'd been thinking he could swim anytime he wanted to, and now he was going to have to depend on Dad to take him.

"Cheer up," Dad told him. "Clipper's Point is an excellent

place to swim. The water is clean, there are lifeguards, and it doesn't cost much."

"Okay," Jake shrugged, and ten minutes later they were in the old green Subaru station wagon, pulling out. Jake adjusted the front passenger seat, looking around. Everything inside the car was familiar—the worn gray upholstery, the shape of the dashboard, the stick shift—but at the same time it looked strange, because he hadn't seen it for so long. Also it was a lot cleaner than he remembered.

He had always thought of it as "our" car, but not anymore. Now it was Dad's car.

Before they reached the highway Jake spotted Adrian, out playing basketball again. "Hang on, Dad," he said quickly. "Can we take Adrian?"

His father stopped the car. "Who's Adrian?"

"That kid over there. He's the one I played basketball with today."

His father studied Adrian for a second. "Oh, I've seen him around. Sure, ask him if he wants to come."

Adrian's response was, "Cool. I just gotta change." In two minutes he was back, wearing swimming trunks and carrying a towel, and both boys got in the backseat of the car.

Jake's dad turned around with a questioning look.

"Dad, this is Adrian Greene. Adrian, my dad, Chris Berry."

"Hi," Adrian said. "Thanks for taking me swimming."

"You're more than welcome," Dad said. "Is this okay with your parents?"

"It's just my dad, and he's working," Adrian said. "But I know he won't mind."

Dad paused for a second. Jake knew he'd rather have clear permission from a parent. "Are you sure?" Dad asked.

"Absolutely." Adrian smiled. "I take care of myself while he's at work. I'm fourteen."

"Okay," Dad said. "We'll have you back by dinner-time anyway. Say five-thirty. Will that be all right with your father?"

"Sure," Adrian said. "That'll be fine."

The station wagon moved out onto the highway, and the wind whipped through the half-open windows.

"Mr. Berry, how do you like staying here?" Adrian said loudly, over the noise of the wind.

Jake looked at him, surprised. Who would ever talk to a grown-up like that? Unless they were trying to kiss up to them.

"I like it fine," Jake's father answered, rolling up his window so as to hear better. "The lake is beautiful, and I'm getting a lot of work done."

"What kind of work do you do?" Adrian asked.

"I teach college-level history."

"Wow. What kind of history?" Adrian really sounded interested, Jake thought.

"American, mostly."

Adrian started talking about something he'd learned in school about the French and Indian War, and he and Jake's father went on for ten minutes, while Jake listened without saying a word. For one thing, what he knew about the French and Indian War would fit on an ant's toenail. For another thing, he was dumbfounded by the boy sitting beside him, conversing in this smooth, ingratiating way with an adult he'd just met. This Adrian seemed to be no relation to the tough kid he had first seen coolly appraising him from his front door, the boy who had sauntered down the steps and passed him the ball, who had played in a fierce competitive silence as though testing the newcomer.

At Clipper's Point they left the car in the parking lot, dropped their towels on the grass near a little kids' playground, and headed for the water. Jake was going to wade in at the nearest place, but Adrian yelled, "Come on, it's better over here," and led the way to a dock that extended far out into the lake. He took off running, and Jake ran after him, all the way to the end of the dock.

Adrian didn't even pause at the end. He flung himself spread-eagled into the air, yelling like Tarzan, and came down with a huge splash. Jake hesitated just long enough to watch Adrian plunge below the surface and bob up again, then leaped.

He came up sputtering, his skin shocked by the cold, but he was grinning too.

Whap—something hit him in the shoulder, bounced off, and floated. A pink splash ball, and in a second he found the source—Adrian. Jake grabbed the ball, treading water, and flung it back. Adrian caught it neatly, and then they were bombing each other back and forth.

Jake was laughing and yelling, letting out all the crazy stuff inside him. He was full of wild energy, as if he'd never get tired. Adrian was the same, only more intense, with less laughter. The battle went on for a long time and yet it went by in a flash, Jake thought as he climbed up the ladder to the dock after calling time-out.

He sat on the edge, feet dangling, and Adrian sat beside him, both of them breathing hard. Puddles formed around them on the gray boards of the dock. The warm boards and the sun beating down felt good after the chilly water.

Jake spotted his father, heading out from the shallows in a smooth crawl stroke. He moved steadily through the jostling kids playing in the water, all the way to the white rope that marked off the swimming area. At the rope he did some kind of flip-turn and headed back.

Jake pointed him out to Adrian. "Look at him. Only my dad would go to a lake and do nothing but swim laps." He swayed mockingly from side to side, droning, "Back and forth, back and forth, back and forth."

"Your dad's smart," was all Adrian said.

"I guess."

A few white clouds drifted along without crossing the sun's path. The lake was a gleaming blue-green, and far out, the sails of half a dozen boats showed up snow-white against it. At Clipper's Point the air was full of kids' shouts and lifeguards' whistles and tinny songs from radios. Little kids were climbing on the playground structures; families sat around picnic tables and barbecue grills; fourth- or fifth-graders were gathered at the lake's edge under a flag that said CAMP ONADAWA; and people of all ages were splashing in the water, while bronze-skinned lifeguards watched from the dock and from tall platforms on shore.

Jake's father swam over to the dock and held on, looking up at the boys. He wiped his face with a dripping hand and said, "Jake, what do you think? You like Clipper's Point?"

"It's great," Jake said. "Can we come here every day?"

"Sure, after I finish my work. I could use a regular afternoon swim. We could work on your strokes too."

Jake made a face.

His father squinted up at him. "What, you want to do nothing but play all the time?"

"All play and no work makes Jake a happy boy," Jake singsonged.

"Is that so? Well, your crawl could stand some improvement, as I remember," his father said. He sounded stern, but there was a cheerful light in his eyes. "How about next time we work on that a little, then play? And we can bring a ball and gloves and play catch, and maybe grill some burgers."

"Cool," Jake said. The summer ahead was looking good, if he could spend time like that with his father, hang around with Adrian, and maybe meet some other kids to do stuff with too.

"Well, back to my laps," his father said, and swam away.

As Jake watched him, a sudden hard shove in the back sent him face-first into the water. He came up choking and gasping as Adrian jumped in beside him. "What's the big idea?" Jake yelled.

"Come and get me!" Adrian yelled back. His thin mouth turned up in a daredevil grin.

Temper soaring, Jake flailed after him. Adrian moved off in a makeshift backstroke, but Jake grabbed his arm with one hand and with the other smacked water hard into Adrian's face.

They lunged again and again, whacking at arms and faces, dashing water at each other's eyes. Then Adrian threw himself at Jake and came down on his shoulder, pushing him under before Jake could grab much of a breath. Adrian's hand came down on his head, the older boy's weight keeping him under while he struggled, his chest clamoring for air.

When at last Jake surfaced, gasping, gulping in the precious air, Adrian backed off, watching him. Jake swam weakly to the dock and hung onto the ladder, staring at Adrian. Had he freed himself by force, or had Adrian let him go? It was impossible to be sure.

"Are you crazy? You almost drowned me!" he yelled.

"Aw, I was just fooling around," Adrian said.

Maybe, Jake thought. But there was a mean edge to Adrian's fooling.

Several days passed before he saw Adrian again. He didn't walk down the street near Adrian's house at all, even though he was sometimes bored and thought it would be nice to play some basketball. He wasn't sure he wanted to hang around with someone who could turn on you like that.

The whole thing was weird. He was used to horsing around with his friends in the pool back in Wendell. That could get rough sometimes—a lot of splashing in the face and shoving someone's head under, or swimming below another boy and pulling him down by the ankle. But none of them—not Stephen or Luke or Carter or any of his friends—would hold someone under the water for more than a second.

He shuddered, and felt the fear and anger rise in his throat all over again, when he remembered how his whole body had screamed for air, and he couldn't get out from under Adrian.

A mean streak, he thought. That's what his mother would say: "That boy has a mean streak."

The first time he could remember her saying that about someone, he'd been in first grade, and he'd pictured a person with a wide stripe across the top of his head and down his back, like a skunk or a badger. He grinned, picturing Adrian that way. But really, he thought, a mean streak was like a stream running through a wide valley, or a streak of lightning cutting through the sky—it was just a small part of what was there.

At least, he hoped it was only a small part of Adrian.

Jake's father hadn't seen the incident, and Jake didn't tell him about it. If he did, Dad might decide to have a talk with Adrian's father, which would be totally embarrassing. Or he might forbid Jake to hang around with Adrian.

No, this was something between him and Adrian, and he would decide for himself whether he wanted to spend time with the older boy. He was angry at Adrian, but still . . . Adrian was a great basketball player, he was older, and he was cool, with his NBA jerseys and his basketball shoes and his totally sure-of-himself manner.

If Adrian turned out to be the only cool guy in Tracktown, Jake didn't want to be kept away from him for the whole summer.

In those few days Jake and his father settled into a routine. After the train woke them around 4:00 A.M., his father made a cup of coffee and went back upstairs to work at his computer for an hour or so. Jake read or listened to music on his CD player with headphones until he fell asleep again. Usually they slept until the 9:30 train woke them. After breakfast Dad worked for a few more hours while Jake read or skipped stones on the lake, watched some TV, or went exploring along the rocky shore and down to the park. Once Dad was done, Jake could use his computer to play games or do some instant messaging with his friends back in Wendell, or he and Dad might go to Clipper's Point for a swim or drive into town for groceries.

One morning Jake just couldn't get back to sleep after the four o'clock train. He lay in bed with the headphones on, switching from one CD to another. For the fiftieth time he wished he had an iPod, but his mom always said not now, maybe for Christmas.

He kept thinking about his father, Adrian, his mother, his friends back in Wendell, the weirdness of being here in Tracktown with his father. The weirdness of Tracktown itself, where people lived on the shore of an enormous lake but couldn't swim in it; where seven houses formed an isolated little neighborhood; where water pollution and the noise of the trains ensured that only people who were almost poor would live here.

The clock on the desk showed 5:05, and he felt no closer to sleep than he had when the ferocious racket of the train had first awakened him. Restless, he decided to go and talk to his father, who was probably working at the computer in his bedroom across the hall. Dad might get annoyed at being interrupted, but not as much as he would during his main work hours, after breakfast.

Quietly he stepped out of his room, across the tiny hall, and into his father's room. But the desk chair was empty, the laptop screen shimmered with all the swirling colors of the screen saver, and his father lay in bed, sound asleep.

For a moment, staring at his father's closed eyes, at the slight rise and fall of the white sheet over his chest, Jake felt abandoned. Then he realized that he could see his father quite clearly, because a dim light was growing in the sky beyond the window. It wasn't black night anymore, it was dawn, and Jake remembered a few times when he was younger, when he and his parents had risen extra early for a trip. Stepping outside the house then, into the cool air, the pale light, the unaccustomed silence of the street, had seemed almost magical. As though the whole world—or at least the neighborhood—was all theirs.

Jake decided he'd do the same thing now.

He went back to his room and pulled on shorts over his boxers. Then he crept down the creaky stairs, found his sneakers and put them on, and slipped out the back door. In the cool air he walked out to the end of the dock. The lake was like the back of some enormous creature of an oiled gray color, slippery-scaly and undulating. Nothing, so far as Jake could see, moved anywhere on its vast surface. Several birds flew over it, dipping and rising; they gave a few harsh cries that made Jake think they must be seagulls, but he couldn't see them clearly. They were gray bird-shapes floating in a gray sky.

He walked along the side of his house, not the side next to the girls' house but the other one, next to the yellow house, where he hadn't seen anyone yet. Then he was out front on the street, where he stood still for a minute or two, gazing around. Tracktown's two streetlights, one right in front of him and the other several houses farther on, were still burning yellow. Over on the highway an occasional car whipped by, headlights gleaming.

Jake walked through Tracktown, down the middle of the tracks. The air was cool, the sky lightening above the trees beyond the highway, the houses blurry at the edges where night still had a hold on them. The first three houses—the yellow one, his own, and the girls' house—were all black and silent. There was a light on in the fourth house, and through an uncurtained window he glimpsed a woman doing something at a stove.

He watched her for a moment, secret as a spy. No one in the entire world knew he was here.

He continued on, poised and alert, feeling nearly as wild as the raccoon he spotted between the rails some distance ahead of him; it turned its piercing eyes on him for a moment before dashing away down the tracks.

Jake thought he would walk to the end of Tracktown, near Adrian's house, and then turn back. He felt like a soldier on patrol, guarding a village. As he passed the fifth house, a light came on in a room upstairs. Ahead, there was no light in the sixth house, no light in Adrian's.

He stepped up onto a rail, looking down at it, arms out for balance, putting one foot in front of the other. When his stride smoothed out and his balance seemed sure, he looked up. And stopped, teetering on the rail with his heart clenched in ice.

A man stood on the street below him, fifteen feet away. A very strange-looking man.

He had long, straggly gray hair, and he wore long pants and a white T-shirt with big stains on it. Around his neck he wore a long winter scarf. He was staring up at the sky with his head tilted far back, and his lips were moving.

Jake needed only a couple of seconds to take in this picture and decide he'd better get out of there, before this creepy guy looked down and spotted him. He tried to turn around on the rail, but one foot slipped and landed in the gravel with an absurdly loud rattle. He glanced back quickly. The man was staring at him, openmouthed.

Jake ran like hell, and didn't look back until he reached his house. There was no one behind him, no one on the street at all. Heart pounding, he hurried to the back door and inside, locking the door behind him. Upstairs, his father still slept. Jake turned on a light in his room and flung himself on the bed, flat on his back.

That man had to be totally insane, Jake thought with a

shiver. The wild hair, the muttering, the staring at the sky. But maybe the strangest part of all was the look on his face when he finally saw Jake. He hadn't looked startled, as anyone would who'd thought himself alone and suddenly discovered a boy standing nearby. He'd looked utterly terrified.

During that first week, the hours while Dad worked, from ten in the morning until about two in the afternoon, sometimes dragged for Jake. The house was so silent, and there was so little to do, aside from reading and watching TV. He wanted to play some basketball with Adrian, but every time he thought of going down there, he remembered what had happened at Clipper's Point, and he stayed put.

He missed his friends back in Wendell, especially Stephen and Luke, whom he'd known since first grade. He even missed his mom, a little.

Sometimes, of course, Dad paused long enough to use the bathroom or make a cup of coffee or a sandwich, and then he would hang out with Jake for a few minutes. But doing anything really fun together always had to wait until two o'clock.

This strictness about work hours sometimes reminded Jake of the last year before his father left, when Chris Berry taught high school history all day and spent every evening and weekend writing his dissertation, either at home or off in some library. A dissertation, he told Jake, wasn't like a paper for school; it was as long as a book, and maybe someday it would even be published.

By that time Chris had finished taking the classes he needed; he'd done that over a period of about a year and a half, going off to evening classes three nights a week, studying on weekends.

"How come you're doing this?" Jake had asked him, more than once, usually because he was upset that his father wasn't going to be around that day for some soccer game or school play or just to help him with homework. And his father always explained, sometimes patiently and sometimes not so patiently, that he was tired of teaching high school, that he wanted to teach college students, with whom a professor could go into so much more depth about all the complex causes of far-reaching events, the interplay of political factions, geography, personalities, ideals.

"I don't have that far to go for a PhD," he would sometimes add. "I was well on my way when I quit, years ago, and this time I'm going to finish."

"Why did you quit?" Jake would ask.

But his father always answered vaguely. "Life has a way of interfering with people's plans," he'd say. Or merely—his blue eyes clouding—"Why does anyone do anything?"

Whatever had happened to his plans back then, clearly nothing was going to stop him this time.

And nothing did. He finished the dissertation and got his degree and started applying for college teaching jobs. Then he was around a bit more, but that turned out to be worse.

Because that winter, when Jake was in fifth grade and his

father was applying for jobs that would start the following fall, Jake slowly began to realize that this new job wasn't going to be located in Wendell, or even in Syracuse or some other place within commuting distance. It was going to be far away.

"So we have to move?" he asked his father one day. It wasn't long after Christmas, and the tree was still standing in a corner of the living room but looking thin and dry. Jake stood beside Dad's desk in another corner of the living room, where Dad sat in his swivel chair, addressing a large tan envelope. There was a printed list of job openings on the desk, and the jobs were in California, Ohio, Texas, North Carolina, Delaware, New Jersey.

Dad put down his pen, and he seemed to take a slow, deep breath before he turned and put his arm around Jake. "You and Mom are going to stay here, Jake," he said gently. "If I get one of these jobs, I'm going to move by myself."

Jake felt as though his heart had stopped, as though everything inside him had turned to stone. Then he began to cry, and Dad held him, and promised that he would visit a lot, and call and e-mail, and told him how this way he'd still have his friends around and wouldn't have to go to a new school.

"And anyway, Jake, it's not till next fall, so let's not get too upset about it, okay?" And because his father's words had made him feel just slightly better than he'd felt in that first terrible moment, Jake had nodded bravely and stopped crying. But there was something heavy inside him almost all the time after that.

Later Jake realized that his mother had known about this long before he had. That whole fall, he remembered, his parents had argued a lot, even though they stopped when he walked into the room. There was constant tension in the air, and his mother was tight-lipped and preoccupied, and often aimed bitter remarks in his father's direction.

"As long as you're still here," she'd say, "maybe you could manage to take out the garbage."

One evening his father picked up his keys and said, "I'm going out for a few minutes," and Mom, who was sorting through a stack of magazines and catalogs, without even looking up said coldly, "Why not?"

Whatever that was supposed to mean.

When Jake and his father left each morning so that Dad could drop Jake off at school before going to his job at the high school, Mom would hug Jake and say good-bye, but she said nothing to her husband and never even looked at him.

"Let's go," Dad would growl, and Jake would follow him out the door, feeling like something was wrong with all three of them, and they'd never be right again.

Jake's mother called one evening while he and his father were in the living room playing chess. Jake didn't really like chess that much, but his father thought it was a game that everyone should know. His father always won, except once in a while when he let Jake win. He pretended he hadn't, but Jake knew he had.

His father answered the phone, while Jake stared glumly at the board, where he had just lost his second knight.

Judging by the side Jake could hear, his parents were having a polite, how-are-you kind of conversation. It didn't last more than two minutes before Chris turned the phone over to Jake and walked away, into the kitchen.

"Hi, Mom."

"Jake! How you doing, big guy?"

"Okay." He could picture her holding the phone in the kitchen back in Wendell, perched on the old-fashioned metal step stool with her feet on the bottom step, next to the bulletin board and the little table that was always cluttered with bills and grocery coupons and notices about soccer or blood drives or collections for the local food pantry. She'd have her elbows propped on her knees, and her shoulder-length sandy hair with the blond streaks—highlights, she called them—falling around her face.

At least that was the way her hair was when he'd last seen her, about a week ago. It might have changed by now. That was because his mom, Lena Berry, was a hairstylist, and she worked in the same shop with her best friend, Denny. She and Denny were always trying something new on each other—a new cut, a new gel, a little color, or a perm or something.

"How is it, being there with your dad?" she asked. "Does he do things with you? Or have you found any friends to hang out with?"

"Well, I found one friend, sort of. This guy named Adrian. And sometimes I go swimming with Dad." Jake stretched the phone cord so he could look into the kitchen, and he saw that his father had gone out the back door and was standing just outside, looking toward the lake.

He lowered his voice and went on. "But it's kind of boring around here. I mean, Dad's always working, and he gets mad if I interrupt him." Just saying it, with his mom sympathetically listening, intensified Jake's complaints.

"Hmm," his mother said. "Well, how much is Dad working? I mean, does he just ignore you all day long?"

There was annoyance in her voice, and Jake tensed up. He knew how quick she was to blame Dad; she'd pounce on any chance to say he was wrong. A twinge of guilt tightened Jake's insides, as though he was betraying his father by complaining about him. And yet, hadn't his father betrayed *him*, by leaving him and his mother and moving away? Shouldn't Dad be making it up to him this summer, somehow?

"It's not really all day," he muttered sullenly. Just because he had a complaint about Dad, that didn't mean he was on her side and against Dad. He didn't want to be on anyone's side.

"Most of the day?"

"He usually stops about two o'clock, and then we go swimming or something."

"Oh." She sounded mollified, in a grudging sort of way, as though Dad wasn't behaving as badly as she'd suspected—or hoped.

It was on the tip of Jake's tongue to say he didn't want to spend a whole summer here, that pretty soon he needed to get back to Wendell and see his friends. But at that moment he heard the back door open and close, heard his father's steps crossing the kitchen, and he closed his mouth. There was no way he could say that in front of his father.

He knew what his mother would say, anyway. That he hadn't been here all that long, that he needed to give it more of a chance, that the whole point of this was for him to be with his father, after so many months without him. That a boy needed a father in the house. And he knew the exact way she'd say it, taking a deep breath first, sounding reluctant but firm, just the way she'd been when they'd first discussed the plan for the summer.

And he had wanted to come, wanted it so so badly. To be with Dad again.

5

Sometimes the little girl next door—Maddy, Adrian had called her—was out playing in her backyard or paddling her feet in the lake. "Hi, boy," she called brightly in her baby voice every time she saw Jake. And sometimes a tall, slender girl with long brown hair sat on their back steps, keeping an eye on her. But the tall girl never said anything, just tossed back her hair, whenever Jake answered Maddy with an embarrassed "Hi."

Nothing more than a narrow strip of weeds separated Jake's yard from the girls'. It looked as though someone had once planted a border of flowers there but had given it up a long time ago.

The dock at the girls' house looked shaky and lopsided, and a few boards were missing. Tied to the dock, and bumping gently against it every time a passing speedboat or Jet Ski spread a rippling wake across the lake, was a small gray boat. It was the bare minimum of a boat, with nothing but two boards to sit on, a skinny outboard motor, and a couple of paddles, a bucket, and a fishing rod in the bottom. So far, Jake hadn't seen anyone use it.

One afternoon as Jake sat on his dock, dangling his feet in the water and wishing for something to do, Maddy and her sister—Jake couldn't remember what Adrian had said the sister's name was—came out their back door. Maddy was holding what looked like an old Easter basket with pink ribbons, which she set down carefully in the yard. The sister sat down on the steps, and Jake looked away, not wanting to be seen watching them, and pretended to be interested in something on the far side of the lake.

Maddy discovered him anyway. "Hi, boy," she said, and he looked around. The sight of him seemed to give her an idea, and picking up her basket, she clambered through the weeds and ran up to him, her blond hair shining in the sun. The tall girl called out in a lazy voice, "You get back here," but she didn't stir from the steps where she sat, and Maddy ignored her.

"Look what I got," she said, holding out her basket.

Jake obligingly looked in. The basket had a dusty-looking blue cloth in the bottom, and on it were two little plastic dolls maybe four inches tall—one dressed as a policeman and one as an ice-skater—and several unidentifiable brown cookies.

"Nice," Jake said, and glanced over Maddy's head to her sister, who was gazing out at the lake with a bored expression, her profile turned toward him, showing her slightly upturned nose and the graceful sweep of chestnut-brown hair tucked behind her ear.

"Want a cookie?" Maddy asked. Without waiting for an answer she was already holding one out to him with a dirty hand.

"Umm," he hesitated. He was slightly hungry, but he wasn't sure he wanted a cookie that had been in that dusty basket and that grubby little hand.

The sister made up his mind for him. "I wouldn't eat that if I were you," she said, standing up and walking toward Maddy and Jake. "She helped me make those last week, and they're hard as rocks. She just likes to carry them around."

"Oh. Well in that case, no thanks, Maddy."

Maddy stamped her foot and turned on her sister. "Allie, you're mean!"

The sister, ignoring Maddy, stood with her hands on her hips and looked curiously at Jake. She wore short, faded blue-jean shorts and a black top with skinny little strings over her shoulders. "How do you know her name is Maddy?"

"I'm psychic."

Maddy stared up at him. "Sy—?" she said, but when no one answered her she wandered back into her own yard, carrying her basket.

"Pleased to meet you, psychic. I'm Allison Meehan."

"I thought you were Allie," Jake said, putting his dripping feet up on the dock and leaning back on his hands, looking up at her.

"That's what most people call me. What do people call you, besides psychic?"

"Jake Berry."

She nodded but said nothing. Then she bent down and picked up a small flat stone, cocked her arm, and sent it skipping across the lake.

"Seven. Pretty good," Jake said.

"Eight," she corrected him. "My record is twelve."

"Seriously? You must practice a lot."

"Well, I've lived here for eight years," she shrugged. A breeze was tossing the ends of her hair, which gleamed in the sun. "Anyway, Mondays and Wednesdays I have to hang around here all day, watching Maddy while my mom and dad are at work. There's not a whole lot else to do."

"Do you get paid for watching her?" Jake asked.

"No," Allie said. She picked up another stone and hurled it, but this one gave only two short hops before sinking.

"That's terrible," Jake said, picturing what it would be like to mind a pesky little kid for two whole days every week. He looked at Maddy, who had dumped the contents of the basket in the yard and sat down to play with the dolls.

"It was a bad rock," Allie said. "Too fat."

"No, I mean about not getting paid."

"Oh." She shrugged again. "My parents don't make much money. They just started their own business—it's a music store that sells instruments, sheet music, things like that. So they work a lot of hours, but they can't afford day care more than three days a week. My older sister, Wendy, works too, but sometimes she takes Maddy on her day off."

Jake looked at her curiously. "Don't you hate spending every Monday and Wednesday like that?"

She dipped her toes in the water, stepped in to a level just above her ankles. "Sometimes," she admitted, kicking the water around a little. "But, you know, it's just the way things are. I get my friends to come over sometimes, or I walk down to the park and meet them there. I have to bring Maddy, but she loves the park, so that's okay."

"Allie, Allie, come look!" Maddy called.

Allie didn't turn around. "In a minute, Maddy." Then she spoke to Jake again. "Are you just here for the summer?"

Jake explained about his dad and renting Sam Weesner's house and going back to Wendell at the end of the summer.

"So Sam and Jackie aren't—" Allie began, but Maddy interrupted.

"Allie, Allie, you have to *look*!" she shrieked.

"Okay, I'm coming." Allie turned toward her sister, calling back over her shoulder, "I'd better look or she'll just keep bugging me."

Jake watched as Allie bent over Maddy, her long hair swinging down like a curtain. Her legs were long too. Kind of pale, he thought, for a girl who lived beside a lake.

She looked up, and he quickly shifted his gaze out to the lake and its far shore.

"Hey, Jake," she said. "You never said how you knew Maddy's name."

"Oh. Adrian told me. You know Adrian?"

"I know every single person in Tracktown—I've lived here for eight years, remember?" She was watching him with arms folded, and again he looked away. "Have you met anyone else yet?"

"No." He jumped down from the dock and picked up a flat stone, juggled it from hand to hand, then threw it. It didn't skip at all, just gave an embarrassing *plunk*. Quickly Jake grabbed a handful of bigger rocks and threw them one by one as far as he could, as if he was throwing a baseball. Then he thought of something to ask Allie.

"Who lives in that house?" he said, pointing to the one on the other side of Sam Weesner's. Its yellow paint was peeling, like most of the paint on Tracktown houses, but there was a solar panel on the roof. It was the first house in the Tracktown row, and beyond it was only a long, narrow stretch of rocks and weeds and train track, leading eventually to the park. So far Jake hadn't noticed anyone there at all—no car, no face at a window, no sound of a voice or a TV.

"Oh, that's Roger's house. I think he's gone on vacation or something. You'll meet him sometime. He's always out in his boat, collecting samples of water from different parts of the lake." She pointed to Roger's small boat, the contents of which were concealed under a tightly fitted vinyl cover. "He's some kind of scientist—an environmentalist, I think. He writes letters to the newspaper about people polluting the lake."

"Does he have any kids?"

"Nope. He lives by himself."

"Oh." Jake went back to hurling rocks, wishing there were more boys to hang around with. Sometime maybe he'd meet Peter, the one Adrian had mentioned—maybe he'd be okay, even though he was younger.

"Got to go potty," Maddy said suddenly.

"Okay, let's go," said her sister, going over to the screen door and holding it open for Maddy.

"Bye, boy," said Maddy.

"Bye, boy," said Allie. "Don't fill up the lake."

"How did you guess my evil plan?" Jake replied in his Darth Vader voice, but the door had already closed behind them.

He threw rock after rock, but the girls didn't come back, and after a few minutes he heard music coming from their house. A radio or a CD, playing something classical that sounded vaguely familiar. It was a piano solo, full of mingled rushing tones that made him think of streams and waterfalls.

He wouldn't have thought a girl like Allie would be into classical music. Whatever "a girl like Allie" meant.

The days grew steadily hotter. Jake's father moved his laptop and his papers and books downstairs to the living room, where it was cooler. Sometimes Jake would read or fool around with his baseball cards in the same room, but that didn't work so well. His father didn't want to be interrupted, and Jake always forgot.

"Dad, listen to this," he'd blurt out, chortling, because he'd just read about Mrs. Salt with her huge rear end like a mushroom up in the air as she leaned over the garbage chute in *Charlie and the Chocolate Factory*, which he was reading for the fifth time at least.

"Not now," his father would murmur, not lifting his eyes from the computer or the book he was reading.

But now Jake was laughing so hard he almost rolled off the lumpy couch. "You gotta hear this—it's so funny. The squirrels just threw Veruca Salt—"

"Jake," his father groaned, looking up at last. "I have work to do. I'll spend time with you later, but right now I want no interruptions unless the house is on fire."

"Okay, okay," Jake would say, still giggling. He'd start reading again, getting totally absorbed, and twenty minutes later it would happen again. He didn't mean to bug his father, but without thinking he'd say something or laugh out loud, and after two or three times Dad would say that he'd better find somewhere else to read.

If he was looking at baseball cards, he'd want to tell Dad something about Hank Aaron or Sammy Sosa, and he'd clamp his mouth shut because he wasn't supposed to interrupt. But then he'd come across something so amazing he'd just have to say it.

"Hey, Dad, did you know Carlton Fisk used to play for the Red Sox?"

And sometimes Dad would get interested and start talking about baseball with him, which was great, except that after ten minutes his father would suddenly remember he was supposed to be working. "Jake, how am I ever going to get work done with you in here distracting me? Out!"

One of those times, when Jake had just been told to clear out of the living room, it was almost noon, so he went to the kitchen and made a turkey sandwich and poured himself a glass of milk. After he ate, he found a piece of paper and a pen and sat down in the little booth again. He made a sign with fat letters, each filled in with circles or zigzags or squiggles, that said TRACKTOWN DINER. He stuck it to the wall with tape, and then wandered out back to the edge of the lake.

The sun was beating down hard, and Jake walked around in a few inches of water, picking up stones and skipping them, watching the rings spread out and disappear. He looked longingly at the green depths, far out, but after what his dad had said about what was in the water, he wasn't about to go any deeper. Not here, anyway. If only he could drive himself to Clipper's Point. It was so unfair, living right next to a lake and not being able to swim in it.

He was sitting on the end of the dock, trying to spot fish in the murky water, when he heard footsteps behind him. Turning quickly, he saw Adrian step onto the dock.

"Hey," Jake said casually.

"Hey," Adrian said, equally casual. He stopped a few feet away from Jake, looking past him to the lake. He was wearing black basketball shorts and a khaki vest with lots of pockets.

Jake shifted around to lean back against one of the posts on the end of the dock so that he had one side to Adrian and one side to the lake. They were silent for a minute.

"It's wicked hot," Adrian said at last.

"Tell me something I don't know."

"Wanna go swimming?"

"Can't. My dad's working. He probably won't be done till about two o'clock."

Adrian's eyes narrowed on Jake's. "What do we need him for?"

"You swim *here*?" Jake said.

"No way, the water's gross here. But if we walk up that way"—he pointed toward his end of the road—"there's good places to swim."

Jake was skeptical. "How far?"

"About twenty minutes."

"Is the water clean?"

"Yeah, it's clean."

Jake gazed out at the lake, where two seagulls skimmed the surface and a Jet Ski roared past. The water looked deep and cold and inviting, and it was too hot to sit here much longer. But did he really want a hot, rocky hike to a swimming place? More important, did he really want to swim with Adrian? What if swimming for Adrian was like the full moon for a werewolf?

Adrian seemed to read his mind. "Come on. I won't jump on you." There was just the faintest hint of a smirk around his thin mouth, but Jake took it as a challenge and instantly made up his mind.

"You do, you die," he said. He got to his feet. "I'm gonna change."

Inside, it took only a couple of minutes to put on his swimming trunks and sneakers, bypass the bottle of sunscreen on the dresser (which Dad would have told him to use), and decide not to interrupt his father to tell him where he was going.

Jake and Adrian walked down the street to the end, then switched to the railroad tracks. For a while the tracks went steadily uphill, close to the highway, while on their left a short stretch of extremely rocky ground descended to the lake. This rocky slope grew steeper as they trudged along, planting each step on a railroad tie. They were sweating in the sun, and their legs prickled with the weeds they sometimes brushed through. Bees droned around blossoms of clover and chicory.

Then the tracks, along with the highway, began to bend to the right, and Adrian stopped. "Now we have to go down," he said.

There was no path. Jake followed Adrian as they picked their way diagonally down the slope, sliding sometimes on loose stones and raising little clouds of bone-dry dust. Jake fell once, scraping his leg.

Finally they reached nearly level ground, close to the lake. Jake stopped. "Why don't we swim here?" he called to Adrian, who was walking ahead.

Adrian didn't turn around or even pause. "There's a better place up this way," he said. Reluctantly, Jake followed. He was hot and tired, and though he wasn't wearing a watch, he was sure they'd been walking a lot longer than twenty minutes.

They were approaching a point of land, so they couldn't see far ahead. The slope of the land was growing gentler, and there were more bushes and even a few skinny trees.

Jake caught up with Adrian at the point itself, where more trees clustered. "Ah, shade! Glorious shade!" he cried, dropping to his knees and flinging his arms around the nearest tree trunk.

"Forget shade," Adrian said.

Jake looked up. "Forget shade? Why?"

"Use your eyes, dodo," Adrian said quietly, staring through the trees, and then Jake stood up and followed his gaze.

The point was the edge of a cove, and the entire cove was lined with a gleaming white sand beach. Jutting into the lake were a long dock and a boathouse with the white hull of a sizable craft visible inside. Beyond the beach was a perfect green lawn, with clusters of pink-flowered shrubs. Jake's eyes swept up the sloping lawn to rest on an enormous house, three stories tall, with picture windows and decks or balconies on every floor.

"Wow," he breathed.

Adrian folded his arms and surveyed the scene. "This," he announced, "is where we swim."

Uneasily, Jake looked from the quiet waters of the cove to the empty windows of the house.

"We'll leave our shirts and sneakers here," Adrian said, bending to untie his shoes.

"Um, I don't know if you've noticed, Adrian—but this is somebody's house."

"Yeah, I noticed."

"Like, this is *so* private property."

Adrian unzipped his vest, slipped it off, and dropped it. "The beach, yeah, but do they own the lake?"

"No," Jake admitted.

"So they can't keep us from swimming in it. Anyway, I've

gone swimming here about fifty times, and there's never any-body home during the day. The only time I saw anybody was after five o'clock."

The water looked soft, deliciously cool, deeply green. All Jake wanted was to plunge in. But he didn't want someone to come out and yell at them, or maybe call the cops.

"Chicken." Adrian smirked, and Jake felt his hot cheeks get hotter.

Without another word Adrian strode off, out of the shelter of the trees, across a short stretch of rocky ground, and onto the white sand. Jake bared his teeth and growled at Adrian's back. Then he wriggled out of his shirt and sneakers, and with one more glance at the blank windows, he followed Adrian.

The water was one swift slap of cold, and then it was heav-enly. They lolled and floated, and Jake loved the feel of the lake sucking the heat from his overheated body, from legs and arms and head. He and Adrian swam lazily over to the dock, where a metal ladder hung down, and climbed up and leaped off.

The first time he got up on the dock Jake looked anxiously back at the house. Nothing moved there. The big windows were still empty, the patio was empty, the lawn was empty of all but the islands of pink flowery shrubs; not even a dande-lion marred its perfect green surface.

Then he vowed, silently, that he wasn't going to ruin this great swim by worrying about the owners of the house. He swore he wouldn't look back again. He turned toward the wide-open lake, ran for it, and jumped as high and far as he could.

Over and over they leaped, in cannonball lumps or spread-eagled wide, in graceful dives or smacking belly flops. Adrian too seemed liberated, really happy, grinning and calling out to Jake as he jumped, and never once trying to pounce on him.

Jake forgot all about the long hot walk, Adrian calling him chicken, the fearsome, unknown owners of this place, even the way Adrian had held him underwater at Clipper's Point. Here, now, was cool and wet and wonderful, and Adrian, his new friend, had brought him here, and they were having a blast.

When the two o'clock train went by, Jake barely noticed. Here the train was just a moderate sound, not the roaring invader it was in Tracktown.

He was starting to tire—they must have been in the water a couple of hours—when Adrian called to him urgently just as he was starting up the ladder.

"Jake! Get down!"

Jake turned a startled face toward Adrian, then, following Adrian's gaze, toward the house. On the patio stood a woman in a long dress, shading her eyes with one hand, staring at them.

Jake slid down low in the water.

"Let's get out of here," Adrian hissed. "Come on, we'll swim over to the point."

The point looked far away, but there was no choice. Jake

pushed off from the ladder, at first swimming at top speed, with Adrian beside him. After a few minutes, though, he had to slow down, and Adrian pulled ahead.

Jake's arms and legs and lungs were all complaining. Gasping, he paused and looked back. The woman was still there on the patio, probably still watching them, but at this distance she surely couldn't identify them. He hoped she hadn't called the police before she came out to the patio.

He swam on, and finally his foot smacked against a stone, and he put his feet down on more stones, and Adrian too stood up, just ahead of him. They stumbled through the shallows around the point, out of sight of the house, and up to dry ground. Then they stood there, breathing hard and grinning at each other. "How cool was that!" Jake crowed. "We did it."

"Yeah." Adrian held out his hand and they smacked a resounding high five. "We swam at the rich people's beach and we didn't get caught."

"Not just a beach," Jake said. "That's the Riviera."

"Yeah, the Riviera. Cool."

Under the trees they sat down next to their shoes and shirts. Jake was pulling his sneakers on when he heard an odd metallic sound and looked up. Adrian was holding a flaming lighter to a cigarette clamped between his lips.

Jake was so surprised, he couldn't say anything. He just watched as Adrian tucked the lighter into one of the pockets in his vest, then leaned back against a tree and blew out a long plume of smoke. He gave Jake a cool, appraising glance. "What's the matter, you never seen anybody smoke before?"

"Yeah, I've seen people smoke before," Jake said defensively. But, he thought, almost all of them were a lot older than Adrian. Besides, smoking was gross. The smell was horrible. And everybody, even little kids, knew it would do nasty things to your lungs and give you diseases like cancer—diseases that could kill you.

But Jake didn't say any of this. Neither of them spoke for the few minutes it took Adrian to smoke the cigarette down to the filter. Then Adrian put on his sneakers, stood up, dropped the butt in the dirt, and stepped on it. He put on his vest, Jake pulled on his T-shirt, and they started up the slope toward the tracks and home.

The steep hillside, with its loose stones and dry, crumbling dirt, was a hard climb. But at last they were on the tracks, walking gradually downhill toward Tracktown.

The heat was still intense, but Jake felt as though it couldn't touch him; his body had been cooled to the core during the hours in the lake. He and Adrian walked side by side, talking about the best water parks they'd ever been to, and then about baseball.

"Yankees bombed the Cardinals Sunday night," Adrian said.

"Yeah, I saw it."

"Me too. Jeter was great."

"I watch all the games with my dad. Which is really cool because at my mom's house she always wants to watch something else, so we have to flip a coin."

Adrian waved away a cloud of gnats. "My dad watches baseball all the time when he's not in his lab," he said. "He has this lab in our basement, and nobody's allowed in there except him. Because some of the chemicals and stuff he works with are really dangerous—you could blow yourself up in there."

"You mean that's his job, working in his lab?" Jake asked.

"Yeah, he gets contracts from the government—the Defense Department, places like that. They pay him to do all these experiments."

"Cool," Jake said. "Is it for, you know, making weapons or something like that?"

"Some of it," Adrian answered, swatting at the gnats again. "He works with these new experimental plastics. He's not supposed to talk about it, but I think some of them are for plastic explosives."

"Wow."

They walked in silence for a minute. Jake was thinking about how cool it must be to have a father doing secret work for the Defense Department.

"You mostly live with your mom, right? In Wendell?" Adrian asked.

"Not mostly—totally."

"Don't you ever go to your dad's place?"

"Not really," Jake muttered. He didn't want to talk about his father. He opened his mouth to say something about the Red Sox, but Adrian, with a sharp stare, questioned him again.

"Haven't you ever even seen where he lives?"

No, said an angry voice in Jake's head. No, I've never once seen the place where my father has lived for almost a year. He's never taken me there. He's never asked me to come. He's made excuses whenever I've asked to visit.

But the voice stayed inside. Outside, Jake looked away from Adrian and talked to the weeds beside the gleaming rail. "Well, it's five hundred miles away. And it's really small. It's just a tiny apartment."

Adrian seemed unconvinced. "Weird," he said.

Jake didn't answer. He picked up a long stick and started fencing with the tallest weeds, thrusting and parrying. "Take that, ye scurvy knave! And that!" He whacked the heads off some daisies, then attacked a thistle, the top of which bent under blow after blow but didn't break.

"Hold it!" Adrian shouted. He came up beside Jake with a rock the size of a loaf of bread in his hands. He held it over the thistle and said, "Die, you dog." *Whump.* End of thistle.

When they came at last to Tracktown, and left the tracks for the street, Adrian said quickly, "I have to do chores. See you later, okay?" And he broke into a run, dashing the short way to his house and disappearing inside without even a wave.

He took off so fast he probably didn't even hear Jake reply, "Okay, see you."

Funny, Jake thought. It looked like Adrian didn't want him to come into the house, or even get a glimpse inside.

When Jake opened the Swiss-cheese screen door, his father was sitting on the plaid couch, the phone in his hand. "I know," he was saying. "I want that—" He broke off, seeing Jake, and then said, in a different voice, "Hang on—the prodigal has returned. I'd better have a talk with him. Mind if I go now, and call you back later?"

As his father was saying good-bye, Jake took off his sneakers just inside the door, wondering who was on the other end of the phone. He was going to ask, but his father spoke first.

"Where have you been? I was starting to get worried about you."

"Oh, sorry," Jake said. "I went swimming with Adrian. We walked a little way up the lake."

"You really should have told me where you were going."

Jake didn't think it was any big deal, but the sun and swimming and walking had left him too tired to argue. "Okay," he shrugged. "Sorry. Next time I'll tell you."

He went to the kitchen, poured himself cold water from the plastic pitcher in the refrigerator, then returned to the living room and sank into the ratty armchair. His father sat on the couch, leaning back, with his ankle crossed over his knee.

"So where did you swim?"

"Just up the lake a little way."

"Far enough for the water to be clean?"

"Definitely. We must have walked for a half hour or maybe even an hour."

"Then you must have been up where all the mansions are."

Uh-oh, Jake thought. "No, not exactly. Maybe it wasn't that far." He took a drink of water. "I mean, we could see a couple of big houses, but where we were swimming it was just all rocky. No houses, I mean." It was sort of true, he told himself. They had swum from the dock to the point, and there weren't any houses at the point.

Jake thought it was time to change the subject. "Who was on the phone?"

"Oh, a friend of mine."

"From the college?"

"Yes." And then it was Chris Berry who changed the subject. "Say, I don't suppose you'd want to go for a swim at Clipper's Point?"

"No way. I'm too tired. I'm just going to chill for a while."

"Hmm." His father rubbed his eyes, ran a hand through his hair. "I could use some exercise, but maybe I'll put it off." He looked at Jake for a moment, almost as if he was going to say something serious. But when he spoke, it was only to say, "So Adrian showed you this place?"

"Yeah, he's been there before."

"You like Adrian?"

"Sure." At the moment he did. It had been a good day, and he didn't want to talk about any of the puzzling things about Adrian.

His father seemed to be waiting for him to say more, but Jake didn't feel like it. He was tired, and his shoulders and face felt hot, so he knew he'd gotten too much sun. He leaned back in the chair and closed his eyes.

"Does he have brothers and sisters?" his father asked.

Jake opened his eyes, surprised he didn't know the answer. "I don't think so. He never mentions any."

"Do you know what his father does?"

"He's a scientist—he works in a lab in their basement."

"Really?" His father seemed to find this slightly strange. "Not at a university, or an industrial lab?"

Jake shrugged. "Adrian says he works at home."

"Hmm," his father said. "Well, I'm glad you found a boy to hang around with."

"Yeah." Jake drained the water glass and eased himself out of the chair. "I'm gonna go upstairs and read for a while."

"Oh. Okay."

As he put his glass in the kitchen sink, his father called, "No more disappearing, Jake. You check with me before you go anywhere."

"Okay," he said, heading for the stairs.

"Why don't you read down here? You can have the couch."

"Maybe later," Jake said, and went on up.

He had an odd feeling that his father wanted something from him, maybe just wanted him to stay. But he was tired, and he wanted his own space.

He settled in the beanbag chair with a fan blowing on him and a book in his hands. After a while he got up to go to the bathroom, and as he stepped out of his room he could hear the faint buzz of his father's voice, on the phone again. Jake paused for a moment, there at the top of the stairs, but he couldn't distinguish any of his father's words.

"You know what's funny about Adrian?" Jake said to Allie the next day. He had just gone to Adrian's house and rung the doorbell, hoping to play some basketball, but nobody had come to the door. He had stood there for a couple of minutes—looking at the blank door, the single front window blocked by green curtains, the litter of odd items around the steps—and then he had walked back toward Sam's house. On the way he'd found Allie sitting on her front steps, helping Maddy squeeze pink Play-Doh into a contraption that pressed it out like strings of spaghetti.

"What's funny about Adrian?" she said.

"It seems like he doesn't want anybody to come in his house."

"What do you mean?" she said carefully. She didn't seem at all surprised by Jake's words; it was more as if she just wanted to hear what he was thinking before she made any comment.

He told her how Adrian had brought water outside instead of inviting him in when they played basketball, and how he'd dashed into his house and shut the door after their swim at the Riviera. And how Adrian never mentioned any family except his father.

A new thought occurred to Jake as he was speaking. "Maybe it's just me," he said. "Have *you* ever been in his house?"

"No."

"Have you ever met his family?"

"Not exactly."

When she didn't continue immediately, Jake snorted and rolled his eyes. "Aren't we mysterious today? How about filling me in, Miss Mysterious?"

Allie paused to admire the Play-Doh spaghetti that Maddy held up to her, and didn't answer until Maddy had gone back to squeezing out more pink strings, singing softly to herself. "Well, I can tell you one thing. It's not just the two of them. There's a girl who lives there—well, a woman really. I think she might be Adrian's sister, but she's a lot older than him. She doesn't go to high school, anyway."

"What about his father?"

"I've never met him, but I think I've seen him once or twice. Only I wasn't sure it was really Adrian's dad that I saw." She hesitated, as though picking her words. "There's something weird about Adrian's father. I think he's there all the time, but he never comes out."

"I know about that," Jake said. "Adrian told me he's a scientist. He spends all his time in his lab, down in their basement."

"Yeah, I heard that too. Adrian says he's some kind of chemist, and he's invented all these valuable formulas."

"Like for weapons—explosives." Jake nodded.

"Maybe. I don't remember exactly. Some kind of special plastics, I think he said."

Jake picked up a tennis ball that was lying near the bottom step and began rolling it down the narrow handrail, trying to get it to roll all the way to the end. It kept veering slightly and falling off.

"Did you ever meet Adrian's sister?" he asked, scooping up the ball in midair with a flourish.

"No, but at least I know what she looks like. I've seen her getting in her car, buying groceries, things like that."

"Doesn't that seem kind of weird? I mean, living this close, and you've never actually met them?"

Allie shrugged. "Not really. Just because we live in Tracktown doesn't mean we all hang around together. And anyway, Adrian hasn't lived here that long—just since January."

"Oh." Jake was surprised; somehow he'd assumed Adrian was an old-timer in Tracktown.

The ball made it to the end and dropped off, landing on the slate below with a dead sort of plop. Maddy, who had been watching intently, grabbed it. "My ball," she said, clutching it with both hands.

"Your ball." Jake nodded solemnly. "Definitely."

■ ■ ■

That afternoon Jake tried Adrian's door again, and this time Adrian was home. They played a long game of basketball, then sat on Adrian's front steps, drinking big cups of ice water. It was nearly six in the evening, and the steps were shaded by the house. They'd seen a few cars pull into Tracktown, as people came home from work. Allie's parents had come home from the music store in their beat-up Chevy Blazer.

Two houses away from Adrian's, the old man was out sitting in his lawn chair again. A boy—smaller than Jake, with dark, longish hair—came out and said something to the old man, then looked over at Adrian and Jake. He waved, and Adrian returned a sloppy military salute. Jake, who had never met this boy, half lifted his arm in a wave. He didn't want to look unfriendly, but it seemed kind of stupid to wave to someone you didn't know.

The boy went inside, and the old man leaned back in his chair, staring off toward the highway.

"Who's that?" Jake asked.

"Peter Glass. And his grandpa. I told you about them."

"Not much. You ever play basketball with him?"

"Once in a while, but he stinks at it. He's little, and besides, he's kind of nerdy. Likes to collect bugs and fossils and stuff like that." Adrian rolled his eyes.

"Oh." Jake thought about this for a moment. To him Peter's collections sounded interesting, but he wasn't going to say that, since Adrian seemed to think they were dumb. "Why does his grandpa sit out there on the porch all the time?"

"No idea," Adrian said, shaking his head as if this was something completely beyond reason.

Jake's stomach was feeling hollow. "Hey, what time is it? I'm supposed to be home for dinner by six."

Adrian looked at his watch, a thick, slightly battered sports watch with a black plastic band.

"You've got three minutes."

Jake stood up. "I'd better go. My dad gets all grouchy if I'm late." He set his cup down on the top step. "Why don't you come have dinner with us?"

"Okay." Adrian too stood up, leaving his cup, and started down the steps.

"Don't you have to tell your dad or somebody?" Jake asked, following. He'd heard rattling noises from inside, possibly kitchen noises, so he knew someone was there.

"Naah," Adrian answered. "I only show up for dinner if I want to."

"Cool," Jake murmured, wishing he had that kind of freedom.

When they got to Sam Weesner's house, Jake led the way into the kitchen, where Chris Berry was chopping broccoli. "Can Adrian have dinner with us?"

"Hello to you too, Jake."

"Hi, Dad," he said in a perfunctory singsong, extra loud. To Adrian he stage-whispered, "He has these strange ideas about *manners*."

Adrian just grinned, and then Dad said, "You're more than

welcome to join us, Adrian, assuming you like tuna salad sandwiches and broccoli."

"Tuna?" Jake groaned.

"That's fine," Adrian said. "I like tuna."

"I thought you were normal," Jake said, staring at him with eyebrows raised. "Come on, let's go upstairs."

"Dinner in ten," his father called after them.

They ate in the little booth in the kitchen. Adrian laughed at the TRACKTOWN DINER sign Jake had made, and suddenly Jake felt childish and wished he hadn't done it.

Just as he had in the car on the way to Clipper's Point, Adrian asked Jake's father all sorts of questions—almost as if he, Adrian, were another grown-up: about his work, how his book was going, what the book was about. If it was any other kid, Jake would have said he was a dork, or he was sucking up. But this was Adrian, and Adrian was cool.

As he thought about this, the conversation took off without him. He chewed his way slowly through his tuna sandwich while his dad answered Adrian—at first out of mere politeness, it seemed, then growing more enthusiastic as Adrian kept asking questions, apparently really listening to the answers.

The book, Chris Berry said, was about Franklin Roosevelt and the media, mainly about some influential journalists and how they covered his presidency. Very detailed, he told Adrian—this would be a book for historians, not the kind of thing kids or even most adults would read.

"But you're really interested in it," Adrian said.

"Sure," Jake's father said. "Because it's part of a bigger picture that's fascinating. Roosevelt had this personality that charmed people, persuaded people, and he used it to bring about tremendous changes in this country. The sound of his voice on the radio, the way he looked in photos, the way his words were reported in the newspapers—all that was incredibly important."

"TV too?" Jake put in.

"No TV in those days—this was the thirties and forties."

"Oh, right," Jake said, feeling stupid.

"He was paralyzed, wasn't he?" Adrian asked.

"Yes, he had polio as a young man and never walked again. But the public was largely unaware of that. He was always pictured behind a desk, or sitting down somewhere. You never saw the wheelchair in the news photos."

"That's pretty amazing," Adrian said.

"All you saw in public," Jake's father said, "was this smiling, handsome, wealthy man—a man who absolutely radiated confidence."

"Cool," Adrian said admiringly.

Jake, watching his friend and his father, was glad when dinner was over.

After they ate, the boys cleared the table and Jake's father started washing the dishes. Jake and Adrian went in the living room, and Adrian saw the chess set on the end table next to the couch. "Hey, you play chess?"

"Sort of," Jake answered, tapping a quick riff with his knuckles on the nearest wall. "But I stink at it. My dad slaughters me every time."

"Want to play?"

"Not really," Jake said, a little uncomfortably. He had a feeling playing chess with Adrian would mean getting slaughtered again. "Want to see my baseball cards?"

"Sure."

Jake pulled out a shoe box that had been tucked away under the end table, and the boys sat down on the couch. Jake was showing Adrian his oldest and best rookie cards when Chris Berry came into the room and started tidying up the papers scattered around his laptop on the rickety coffee table.

Adrian looked up. "Mr. Berry, would you play me in chess sometime?"

"You can call me Chris, you know. Sure, I'll play you sometime." He put some of the papers in a box. "I can't get Jake to play with me that often."

Jake rolled his eyes. "He thinks chess is the greatest game ever invented," he said to Adrian.

"Well, it is, isn't it?" Adrian said seriously, turning to Chris. "I mean, there's so much strategy involved, and it's so complicated. Every game's different."

"Right, absolutely," Chris Berry said. "Do you get to play much, Adrian? With your dad, or your friends?"

A shadow crossed Adrian's thin face, vanishing so quickly Jake wasn't entirely sure he'd seen it. "Oh, I used to play with my dad a lot, but he's been too busy with his experiments lately."

"How about your sister?" Jake asked.

Adrian looked startled. "Stepsister," he said quickly. "How did you know I have a stepsister?"

"Allie told me."

"Oh." Adrian still looked slightly unnerved. Jake wondered if the stepsister was really weird or something; could that be why Adrian didn't invite people in?

"Well, anyway," Adrian went on, "she doesn't know how to play chess. Most of my friends don't either, so I don't get to play much."

"How old is your stepsister?" Jake's father asked.

"Twenty. Her name's Miranda."

"Is she in school somewhere?"

"She goes to Henrikson." That, Jake knew, was a community college a few miles away. "But she doesn't go in the summer," Adrian continued. "She has a waitress job at a restaurant in town."

Jake was flipping through his cards. "Look—here's A-Rod, when he played for the Rangers."

Adrian looked, but then he turned back to Jake's father, who had just picked up a piece of paper from the floor and seemed about to leave the room. "Could we play a game of chess right now?"

Chris Berry looked interested, but he hesitated. "Well, it's a two-person game, and there are three of us."

"You wouldn't mind, would you, Jake?" Adrian said eagerly. "I never get to play chess."

"Oh, all right," Jake said, trying to hide his annoyance. Adrian was supposed to be hanging out with *him*, not his father.

"You could watch," his father suggested. "You might pick up some pointers."

"Oh boy," Jake drawled, rolling his eyes. "Can I use the computer?"

"Okay," his father shrugged.

"Cool." Jake slid down the couch, pulling the laptop to one end of the coffee table, while his father took the armchair across from Adrian, who was already setting up the chess game at the other end of the table.

They had barely started when the crescendo of the approaching train began. Jake glanced at the clock on the computer—7:06. By now he was getting familiar with the sound and feel and sight of the train, four times a day—the trembling of the house, the rattles and squeals and whistle blasts that swallowed up every other noise. Nobody got up, but all three of them stared out the window for as long as the huge cars rushed past.

The train stopped everything, four times a day. While it roared through Tracktown no one could hear a TV or music or a voice; no one could talk or sleep or read or think. Everybody's life, Jake thought, was on hold while the train passed through.

A few minutes later he was absorbed in a stalking-and-shooting game, one that his father had reluctantly allowed him to install on the computer. But—even though Jake's eyes were glued to the screen and his fingers were constantly working with what he liked to call his lightning reflexes—his ears were taking in the quiet conversation to his right. He heard his father say "Good move," in a tone of real respect. He heard the occasional "Gotcha," a laugh, a mock groan. It sounded like his father and Adrian were having a really good time.

When the game ended, Adrian proposed a second one, but Jake's father said, "I think one's enough for tonight." He stood up and stretched. "How about some popcorn?"

Then Jake shut down the computer, and the three of them listened to music and ate popcorn and talked about music and baseball and school. Finally Jake's father said, "Time to break it up, guys. Some of us have to get up in the morning."

Moths fluttered around the light over the tiny front porch as they all said good-bye. Jake's father turned back inside, but Jake, after flipping off the light, lingered for a minute on the top step as Adrian moved down to the street. There Adrian paused and pulled a small box out of the pocket of his shorts.

"Hey, Jake," he said quietly, taking out what Jake could now see was a cigarette. "Your dad is a good chess player."

"Yeah," said Jake.

Adrian clicked his lighter and it flared yellow-orange in the darkness, then went out, leaving the glowing coal of the cigarette.

"Well," he said, blowing out a long puff of smoke, "see you later."

"Yeah, later." Jake turned toward the house, but paused with his hand on the screen door's knob, looking back. Adrian was walking away with just a trace of a swagger, the cigarette glowing at his side, then disappearing as he lifted it to his lips and reappearing to the side, accompanied by a delicate fan of smoke. The reflective stripes on his sneakers glittered in the light of the street lamp.

Jake went inside and locked the door. His father had already gone upstairs and was in the bathroom. Jake too went up the creaking stairs, and he lay on his bed in semidarkness, with only a shaft of light from the landing.

What was it about Adrian? Smoking was stupid—everybody knew that. And yet there was something so *cool* about it, at least the way Adrian did it, walking away alone in the dark, his only company that little touch of fire and smoke. Adults might say smoking was bad, but they weren't stopping Adrian. And he was really athletic, even if he did smoke, so it must not be hurting him much.

Maybe the most amazing thing about Adrian was how *free* he was—he didn't have to report to anybody, or be home any particular time. Jake doubted that anybody ever hassled Adrian about dumb things like doing his homework or brushing his teeth. As far as Jake could tell, Adrian could do just about whatever he wanted.

In fact, Adrian didn't seem to need grown-ups at all. There

was just this one odd thing—he seemed to actually want Jake's father's company. Wanted to play chess with him, to have conversations with him about his work. And Chris Berry had seemed to like Adrian too. Jake thought of the way they'd talked about history, the way they both loved chess. He wondered if his father would have liked a son like Adrian. More than a son like Jake.

CHAPTER
8
I I I   I I I I I

The next day around mid-morning there was a knock on the door. Jake was still in his boxers, eating a bowl of cereal at the booth in the kitchen. He'd had a hard time falling asleep the night before, and had drifted off again after the 9:30 train.

At the knock he looked down at his green plaid boxers and hoped that it wasn't Allie. He knew Dad wouldn't answer the door; he was working upstairs. By leaning precariously far out to the side of the booth, holding onto the table, Jake could just see the screen door; on the other side of it was Adrian. With a sigh of relief Jake got up and let him in.

"Hey, it's a good thing you're not a girl," he said. "Don't want any girls to see my undies."

"Yeah, they might puke," said Adrian, and Jake faked a punch to his ear. "Put some clothes on, dude. We've got things to do."

"We do? Well, wait till I finish my cereal." He went back to the kitchen and Adrian followed.

Adrian watched, leaning against the sink, as Jake shoveled

in heaping spoonfuls of Corn Chex. "You got any other kind of cereal?" he asked.

"Maybe," Jake said. "Look in that cabinet right next to you."

"Crap," said Adrian, nudging things around in the cabinet. "What's with all this *healthy* stuff? Don't you have any, like, Cap'n Crunch or something?"

"Naah, my dad won't buy sugary cereal. You know what I'd like to try, though?"

"What?"

"Chocolate-Frosted Sugar Bombs."

"Oh yeah," grinned Adrian. "*Calvin and Hobbes.* That's what Calvin eats all the time. Where are the bowls?"

"Next cabinet, to the left. Spoons are in the drawer right below it." He swallowed a bite of cereal. "Hobbes is so cool. Like the way he's totally real except when other people are around, and then he's just a floppy stuffed tiger?"

"Yeah, Hobbes is cool." Adrian sat down in the booth across from Jake and poured himself Corn Chex and milk.

"And you know what's great about Calvin?"

"What?" said Adrian through a mouthful of cereal.

"He gives his dad ratings. Like grades."

"Not grades—rankings. It's a public opinion poll. Like when they ask people who they'll vote for for president."

"Well anyway, whenever he won't let Calvin do things, Calvin tells him he's really going down."

Jake finished eating and bounced over to the sink to put his bowl in. Since Adrian had arrived he'd felt wide-awake and ready for action. "Hey, didn't you say we have things to do? Like what?"

"Mmm, you'll see." Adrian finished his cereal and slid out of the booth. "Let's go see if Allie's around."

"Gotta get dressed," Jake said. He took the stairs two at a time, and in half a minute he was back downstairs wearing shorts, a T-shirt, and flip-flops. He figured he'd tell Dad later, if they actually went any farther than next door. Adrian was still in the kitchen, looking at the calendar on the wall, and his bowl was still on the table. Jake's father hated having dirty dishes left on the table, and Jake almost told Adrian to put it in the sink, the way he would have told Stephen or Luke back in Wendell. But this time he just did it himself.

When he turned from the sink Adrian was watching him impassively. Jake wondered if Adrian thought he was some kind of nerd.

The sun beat down on Allie's front steps, where Jake stood while Adrian knocked. Behind the screen door, the main door was half open, and music could be heard, piano music again, but something jazzier than before. The music stopped, and Allie appeared behind the screen. She didn't open it, just stood there with her arms folded. Her rich brown hair swayed slightly around her shoulders.

"Hi," Adrian said cheerfully, and Jake gave a little wave.

"Hi." She was looking at them curiously.

"Could we borrow your boat for a while?" Adrian said.

"What for?"

"Just for something to do. I want to show Jake around—go along the edge of the park and some other places."

"Oh. Well, it's my dad's boat, and I'm not sure he'd like me lending it out."

"Oh, come on—just for a little while?" Adrian said. "We won't hurt it or anything. We just want to do a little sight-seeing."

"Hmm." Stalling, she looked at Jake. "Did you forget how to talk or something?"

He moved his mouth silently, shrugged, made elaborate gestures with his hands.

"I see," she said, eyebrows raised.

"Come on, Allie cat," Adrian implored. "Please please pretty please?"

Still she took her time, considering. "Well, I guess it would be okay as long as I went with you."

"Cool," Adrian said.

She paused before adding, "That means Maddy too. I can't leave her here by herself."

"Maddy?" Adrian exclaimed, eyes and mouth wide with outrage. "We have to take a little baby?"

"No Maddy, no me," Allie said firmly. "No me, no boat."

"Sheesh," he muttered.

"Well, if you'd rather skip the whole thing, that's okay with me," Allie said. "I mean, I'm kind of busy anyway."

"No, no, let's do it," Adrian said, still sounding disgruntled. "Go get Maddy and let's get going."

"Sure," Allie said calmly. "Right after I finish practicing."

Adrian opened his mouth, but she didn't give him a chance to argue. "I'll be out in twenty minutes," she said, and disappeared into the back of the house, leaving the boys staring through the screen door at an empty room.

Jake found his voice. "Practicing? That was her playing the piano?" he asked in astonishment, and Adrian nodded. "Holy samoly. Nobody our age is that good."

"You mean you've never heard her?" Adrian said, a little sourly. "All she does is practice."

"I guess I heard her a bunch of times, but I thought it was a CD," Jake said wonderingly.

As the music drifted out the door—slow and tentative at first, then swelling—Adrian sat down on the top step and took a pack of cigarettes out of his shorts pocket. Jake sat down beside him. They listened in silence for a while, staring out across the street and the tracks and the highway to the green hillside beyond it. Adrian puffed on his cigarette and Jake tried to lean away—but not too obviously—from the smelly, drifting smoke.

A lime-green pickup truck turned in off the highway and rattled down the street toward them, and for a crazy second Jake had an impulse to jump up and hide Adrian's smoking. But Adrian didn't seem to feel the slightest need to hide; if anything, he lifted the cigarette to his lips with a bit of a flourish as the truck approached. The words VEGGIE POWERED DIESEL were stenciled on the side of the truck. The driver, a young man with blond hair and a short blond beard, waved as he drove past. He stopped where the road stopped, at the end of the street.

"Is that Roger?" Jake said. "Allie told me a guy named Roger lives in that house."

"Yeah, that's our neighborhood hippie. Mister Vegetarian Veggie-Power. Save-the-lake Roger."

Jake laughed, although he was curious to know if this Roger was actually doing something to clean up the lake. It looked as though it needed some saving, at least at this end.

The music turned sad and wistful, and maybe that was why Jake thought of his mother, and then wondered about Adrian's mother, and why Adrian never mentioned her.

"Hey, Adrian," he said. "Do you ever see your mom?"

Adrian's hand, on the way to his mouth with the cigarette, jerked once, and there was something in his face before he looked away, drawing on the cigarette before answering.

"Sure, I see her pretty often. She lives in New York, in Manhattan. She's an actress."

"Wow. Is she famous?"

Adrian smiled. Already he seemed at ease again, as though whatever had bothered him about Jake's question had vanished. "Well, she's not movie-star famous. She's a stage actress. If you lived in New York and went to Broadway plays you'd know her name."

"What's her name?"

"Susannah Landon."

Jake hadn't heard of her, but then, he'd never been to a Broadway play. "She must be really beautiful, huh?"

"Yeah, she is. She's got really long blond hair."

"Does she ever come here to visit?"

"Not much. She doesn't get along with my dad. Besides, she's really busy. Directors are always after her to be in their plays."

"Wow," Jake said again. "That's so cool." He didn't want to mention that his own mother was just a hairstylist. He thought of the little shop in an old shopping center in Wendell, where his mom and Denny and a couple of other women worked. When you walked in, a bell over the door jangled, and you were greeted with the strangest assortment of smells, sweet and flowery, with harsher chemicals mixed in.

Men, women, and children all came there for haircuts, and when Jake was younger he loved the special occasions when he got his own hair cut there. Most of the time his mom cut his hair at home, with him sitting on a stool in the kitchen. But now and then she brought him to the shop, where all the women made a fuss over him, and Denny gave him candy, and he sat on a special pillow in one of the big chairs. His mom pumped the chair up high, and he could watch her and everyone else in the big mirror.

Now, of course, he was much too old for the special kid treatment, but the oldest of the women still acted like he was about six, which made him furious. Besides, the whole place was just too girly, with the flowery smells and the worn copies of *Oprah* and *Cosmopolitan* and *Self*, and usually an old lady or two in curlers under the big bonnet dryers. The women who worked there swished around, snipping and sweeping, laughing and joking with the customers, completely at home in their world.

It definitely wasn't Jake's world. These days, he only let Mom cut his hair at home. And when he had to go to the shop, like when he had to meet Mom after school to go to the dentist, he set his jaw and slumped his shoulders and said hardly a word, and got out of there as fast as possible.

Ugh. Why couldn't his mother do something cool, like Adrian's mother? Or at least work in a nice office somewhere, be a lawyer or something. It must be amazing to have an actress mother and a scientist father. Jake's mother spent all day in this weird female place, and his father spent his work time inside his head, in a world Jake had no idea how to enter.

The piano stopped—but only for a second. Then Allie played the same phrase over and over, slowly, then faster, as if she needed to work on it, though Jake couldn't hear anything wrong with it.

Adrian ground out his cigarette in the dirt. "Come *on*, Allie, wouldja?" he muttered.

When, finally, Adrian, Jake, Allie, and Maddy stood on the dock looking down at the boat, they were all wearing the orange life vests that Allie had handed them. She said it was her father's rule; you couldn't be on the boat without one.

Adrian and Jake had rolled their eyes, looked at each other, and silently agreed that arguing would be futile.

The boat was made of gray-green fiberglass and knocked gently against the padded side of the dock as the water moved under it. On the sides and the gently pointed bow, metal cleats flashed in the sun.

Allie climbed in and lifted Maddy down to sit beside her on the bench seat in the stern. Adrian stepped in next, and then Jake, whose foot came down too near the side and nearly tipped the boat. He grabbed the dock to steady himself and the boat, then sat next to Adrian on the front seat, facing Allie.

Allie had to yank on the starter cord three times, pressing the choke button, before the sputtering motor finally caught and eased into a throbbing hum.

"You don't even need a key to start this thing?" Adrian said.

"No," Allie told him. "This is about the most basic little motor you can get."

They moved slowly away from the dock, guided by Allie's hand on the tiller. As soon as they were a few feet out she speeded up, and the bow lifted a little, bouncing over the waves, the wind blowing everyone's hair back. Jake was grinning and so was Adrian, both of them twisted around on the seat to face forward, into the wind. Behind them Maddy crowed delightedly.

Jake knew they weren't really going very fast, not compared to the red speedboat he could see racing far out in the center of the lake, and yet the feeling was wonderful—everything so windy and bright and moving, the day suddenly full of excitement and possibility.

Allie took them straight out across the lake, jolting over the wake of the red speedboat. The farther out they went, the larger the lake seemed, and the slower and smaller their boat felt, until Jake thought they were like some buzzing insect on the vast surface.

Then, slowly, the opposite shore drew nearer. Jake was curious about a large boat at a dock dead ahead, but he couldn't see it clearly at this distance. He stared at it intently for long minutes, but their approach was so slow that he still couldn't bring it into focus. He had to look away and shake his head, then look toward it again to detect any progress.

When they were still some distance from the shore, Allie began to bear left and cruise along parallel to it. Jake and the others all stared at the houses and boats and docks, the people swimming and canoeing and sailing, or lying on docks in the sun. The houses and boats here weren't as grand as what Jake and Adrian had seen at the "Riviera"—a lot of these looked like cottages rented out for the summer—but they were still infinitely finer than anything Tracktown had to offer.

Adrian seemed to be thinking along the same lines. "See all that?" he said to Jake. "Now you know why Tracktown is the slum of the lakeshore." Jake grinned, but he could see from the tight line of Adrian's mouth that it wasn't a joke to him.

"Oh, come on," Jake said. "Tracktown's a little run-down, but it's not a slum."

"Easy for you to say. You're just here for the summer."

Jake's only answer was a noncommittal shrug, but he froze in the middle of it. Uh-oh. He hadn't told his father he was going out in the boat. He didn't want Dad to be mad at him, especially so soon after he'd promised to ask before going anywhere. Well, he'd just have to hope they got back before Dad took a break and noticed that Jake wasn't around.

And, he realized suddenly, he'd also have to hope that Dad hadn't just happened to glance out the window at the very moment his son had gone zooming off in a boat with a bunch of other kids. That would not be good. He grimaced to himself and pulled the straps of the life jacket tighter.

"I see a fish! I see a fish!" Maddy shouted, leaning perilously over the side of the boat. Allie had to grab her to keep her from falling out.

Then they were curving left again, and Allie pointed out a cove where her father liked to fish, and that was where Mayfield Park began. She steered them in close to the shore, where bent old willow trees dipped their weeping branches almost into the lake. Then she shut off the motor and tilted it forward so the propeller wouldn't scrape the bottom, and they coasted slowly to land.

When the bow grated on pebbles, Adrian jumped out and pulled it farther up. Jake climbed out too, his flip-flops splashing through a few inches of water, followed by Allie, who lifted Maddy and deposited her on dry ground. All of them quickly stripped off the life jackets, Allie crouching to unfasten Maddy's.

Jake helped Adrian pull the boat completely out of the water, and then he straightened up and looked all around. They were in a grassy area with a few scattered trees, benches, and picnic tables. Beyond it was a road, and then a playground and a couple of tennis courts. Though the spot where they stood was quiet, sounds from all over the park mingled in the air—the pops of rackets against balls, the shrieks of small children on the playground, the greedy squawks of seagulls farther along the shore, surrounding a woman who was tossing them scraps of bread.

Near the road two boys were throwing a football, going out for long passes, and Adrian and Jake watched them. One, a thin black boy, yelled something to the other, then hurled the ball. The second boy—sandy-haired, wide-faced, and stocky—leaped spectacularly for it, pulled it into his chest, and went sprawling in the grass. In an instant he rolled over and jumped to his feet, pumping the ball up and down. "I got *skills*! You see that?" he yelled, doing a comical end-zone dance. The black boy hooted with laughter.

"Yo, Flavin!" yelled Adrian.

The stocky boy looked over and waved, and Adrian said to Jake, "Come on, I know these guys." The two of them sauntered over.

"Flavin, you caught a ball. I can't believe it, man," Adrian said.

"I've been teaching him, but he's kinda slow," said the black boy.

"You wish," Flavin snorted. He looked curiously at Jake and nodded. "Hey."

"This is Jake," Adrian said. "He lives near me, just for the summer."

Flavin nodded again. "Ben Flavin."

The black boy gave a little wave. "Michael Otis."

"Hi," Jake said. They were both taller than Adrian, which made them considerably taller than Jake. He guessed they were fifteen, maybe even sixteen.

Michael looked over toward the shore, where Allie was watching Maddy, playing at the edge of the water near the boat. "Hey, is that how you got here? In Allie's boat?"

"Yeah," Adrian said.

Ben Flavin grinned broadly. "I knew it. She definitely likes you, Greene. She thinks you're hot."

"Yeah, she never gave *me* a ride in her boat," Michael chimed in.

"You guys are full of it," Adrian said. But he looked slightly flushed, and pleased too, Jake thought. For some reason the look on Adrian's face irritated him.

Then, in a half-second flash, he saw himself standing there shyly saying nothing, and that wasn't Jake Berry. He shook off the irritated feeling and dived right in. "Actually, guys," he said, straight-faced, "I'm the one she likes. She told me I'm wicked cool. Adrian, buddy, I hate to break it to you, but she thinks you're, like, *dishwater*."

Adrian cuffed the top of Jake's head—"What a load of crap!"—and Michael and Ben hooted.

"Hey, you guys want to throw a few?" Michael said.

"Sure," Jake said, though he glanced around for Allie. She was heading for the playground with Maddy, so he supposed she wasn't in a hurry to leave.

Flavin was watching her too. He shook his head. "Too bad she has to babysit that kid all the time."

"I don't think she minds that much," Jake said.

"*I* mind," said Flavin, delicately licking his upper lip. "A girl like that should be a little more *available*."

"Oh. Yeah." That was all Jake could think of to say.

The four boys fanned out and started tossing the ball around. Jake was having a good time, but it wasn't long before he started worrying that his father might stop work for lunch soon, and then he'd notice that Jake had disappeared.

Jake hated having his father angry at him. Right after Chris Berry had moved away, Jake had lain awake at night, lots of nights, remembering all the times he'd done something wrong and made his dad angry. Over and over he'd relived those times, pounding his pillow until he broke into a sweat, or tears. Wishing he'd done things differently. Wondering whether his parents would have stayed together if only they'd had a better son.

Finally he called over to Adrian, "Hey, what time is it?"

Adrian caught Michael's pass and drilled it to Flavin before glancing at his watch. "Twelve twenty-five."

Uh-oh, Jake thought, and fumbled a pass from Flavin. He scrambled after the ball, grabbed it, and called to Adrian, "I have to get back pretty soon."

"What's your hurry?"

He didn't want to explain. "I'm just supposed to get back," he said irritably. Adrian said nothing, just faked in his direction, then shot the ball to Michael.

In a few minutes Allie wandered over, trailed by Maddy, and Jake dropped out of the game to walk toward them.

"So you met Michael and Ben," Allie said, pushing back her long hair. In the bright sun it was so much more than brown, gleaming with touches of red and chestnut and gold.

"Yeah. They're pretty good with a football."

For a moment she gave them that studying glance of hers,

then looked back at Jake. "They're all about football, that's for sure."

Maddy came up and leaned against Allie's leg, twirling a bedraggled, long-stemmed dandelion.

"Do you think we could go back soon?" Jake said. "I kind of need to."

"How come?"

"I forgot to tell my dad where I was going." He noticed how easy it was to say that to her, and how he hadn't wanted to say it to Adrian.

"Oh, okay. Let's go back then," she said. "I'm ready."

"I don't think Adrian is."

"He's not driving, though, is he?" she smiled. "Hey, Adrian! Time to go."

Adrian glanced over at them, then talked to the other boys for a moment before walking over to Jake and Allie.

"I'm gonna hang out here for a while," he said. "Those guys will give me a ride home."

"Michael got his mom's car again? He doesn't even have a license," Allie said.

"Who cares? He looks old enough. Anyway, how come you have to leave?"

"Jake needs to go home. His dad doesn't know where he is."

She said it as though it was the most normal, reasonable thing in the world, but Jake really, really wished she hadn't said it at all. A sardonic smile played on Adrian's lips, and

Jake could feel his face getting hot. He told himself contemptuously that he was like a little kid compared to Adrian, always having to ask permission to do anything or go anywhere, always afraid his father would get mad.

Adrian made no comment, though. "Okay, see you later then. Thanks for the boat ride, Allie cat."

When they got back to Allie's dock they saw a young woman walking toward them, between Jake's house and Allie's. She was thin, with shoulder-length hair so dark it was almost black, and from the look of her skin, she spent a lot of time in the sun. She walked quickly toward them, one hand fiddling with the gold necklace at her collarbone.

Jake, Allie, and Maddy had climbed out of the boat, and Allie was tying it up. Jake glanced over at his house; his father was nowhere in sight.

"Hey, you guys seen Adrian anywhere?" the young woman said, stopping at the end of the dock.

"Yeah, we just left him over at the park," Jake answered.

"What the hell is he doing over there?" she burst out—as if it was *his* fault, he thought indignantly. He just stared at her. She kept fiddling with the necklace, which had several charms on it, in a nervous way that reminded him of some twitchy little squirrel or chipmunk.

"We went over in the boat," Allie explained in her calm voice, "and we ran into some friends of his. He wanted to stay and play football with them."

"Why am I not surprised," the young woman said bitterly.

"You're his sister, right?" said Allie.

"Stepsister," she said. Just like Adrian, Jake thought—she sounded like she wanted to get that corrected, fast.

"What's your name?" Allie asked.

"Miranda. Miranda Lowery."

"I'm Allie. This is Jake."

Miranda didn't say anything, just nodded. She stared out across the lake toward the park, though it was impossible, at this distance, to make out anything smaller than the willow trees. Her face, Jake thought, might have been pretty except that there was something hard about it, something tough and bitter that seemed to go far deeper than the anger of the moment. Her brown eyes narrowed against the glare of the sun.

Allie took off Maddy's life jacket, and the little girl toddled off into the yard. Then, removing her own, Allie piled up all four jackets on the dock before looking at Miranda again. "If you really need him, I can take you over in the boat."

"No thanks. He wouldn't come back anyway," she said, and Jake thought she was probably right about that. "The jerk— he promised me he'd help clean up. Swore up and down he'd be home at eleven. The place is a damn pigsty and he won't lift a finger." Her mouth was a tight line, and her eyes shifted restlessly from the park to Jake to Allie. "I finally told him I wouldn't drive him anywhere for a month if he didn't do it today. So I won't. He can get on his knees and beg me, and I'm not driving him anywhere. He wants to go somewhere, he can walk."

While she was talking, the back door of Jake's house opened and his father came out. Anxiously Jake watched as his father approached; he couldn't tell whether Dad was angry or not.

"There you are," Chris Berry said. "I was wondering." He didn't *sound* angry, Jake thought, relieved.

Miranda and Allie turned toward him, and he said hello.

"Allie, right?" he said, and she smiled and nodded. "But I don't think I've met you," he said to Miranda.

"Miranda Lowery," she said, still sounding sullen.

"Adrian's stepsister," Jake said.

"Oh yes. Nice to meet you." Chris Berry held out his hand, and Miranda shook it briefly. "I'm Jake's dad."

"Nice to meet you," she said dully, and gazed out toward the park again.

Jake's father looked at the pile of orange life jackets, which he seemed to have just noticed, and said, with a touch of surprised concern, "Jake, did you just go for a boat ride?"

"Uh, yeah," he said, hoping he didn't sound nervous.

Allie spoke up quickly. "I hope you don't mind that I took him. We all wore life jackets the whole time—that's my dad's rule. He lets me take friends out in it as long as we wear life jackets and I do all the driving."

There was something so calm and grown-up about Allie, Jake thought. Any adult would trust her—as his father apparently did, because he just said, "Those sound like good rules to me."

■ ■ ■

That night after dinner Jake's father took him to a movie at a small theater in town. The theater wasn't crowded, and they got a big bucket of popcorn and sat in the center section, five or six rows from the front, exactly where Jake always liked to sit in movies. They whispered through the previews about what looked good and which movies Jake had already heard about, and groaned at one that looked really stupid.

On the way home, sitting in the front seat beside his father, Jake leaned back contentedly, watching the approaching headlights and the drift of light and shadow over the dashboard. The movie had been only so-so, but Dad had been nice, and it had felt good to do something with him. He thought maybe when they got home he'd call Mom and tell her about it. She might want to hear about the movie, and she might like Dad better since he'd done this for Jake. Maybe—a new idea struck him like the cheerful ring of a bell—he could ask Mom to visit them for a couple of days.

As they turned from the highway onto Tracktown's short, nameless road, their headlights swept across the rough slope at the end of it, where Jake and Adrian had started their trek to the Riviera. And there, sitting on the ground with his hands on his knees, was the same strange, wild-haired man that Jake had seen when he'd gone out at dawn. The man ducked his head away from the glare, but in the seconds the headlights took to pass over him Jake got a good look at him. He was still wearing the long scarf around his neck.

"Dad, who's that weird guy?" Jake almost shivered, there was something so creepy about the man's looks, about the way he sat there alone in the dark.

"I don't know," his father frowned. "He must live around here—I've seen him once before."

"So have I."

"You have? Well, steer clear of him. He may be harmless, but he certainly doesn't look normal. If you see him again, head for home. And don't go wandering around after dark."

"I never go wandering around after dark."

"Well, good. Keep it that way."

His father's commanding tone, along with the sight of the creepy stranger he'd come to think of as the scarf man, combined to dampen Jake's mood, and as he entered the house he thought maybe he wouldn't call his mother after all.

But his father had hardly closed the door behind them when the phone rang, and when Jake answered, it was Lena Berry.

"Hi, honey," she said. "How's my Jake?"

"Good."

"Good and what else?" his mom asked. Jake could picture the way she grinned saying it. She always prodded him to tell her a little more, teasing him about his one-word answers.

"Good and . . . we just went to a movie." He flopped down in the big armchair, legs stretched out.

"Who, you and Dad?"

"Yeah. We saw *Spiderman 3*. It wasn't that great, though."

They talked about movies for a while, and then Jake told her about going to the park in Allie's boat and hanging out with Adrian and his friends.

"Hey, Mom," he said, and hesitated. "It's pretty nice here. You know, with the lake and all. Maybe . . . maybe you could come visit. Like, for a day or two."

His father, sitting on the couch and looking at a magazine, jerked his head up and stared at him. Jake couldn't quite read his expression, and quickly shifted his eyes away.

His mother didn't answer at once, and he hurried to fill up the silence. "If you wanted to, I mean."

"Oh, Jake," she sighed. "I'd love to see you. I really miss you. But I don't think it would work for me to visit. That's— well, that's just not the way your father and I are doing things right now."

"Oh," he grunted, to keep the disappointment out of his voice.

"Anyway, I'll be out of town all next week. I'm going to the Jersey shore with Denny."

"You are? You're going to the beach?" he said, envy creeping into his voice. He felt his father's eyes on him, and didn't look.

"Yeah," she said with another sigh, and he imagined her pushing back the sandy-blond hair the way she always did. "I haven't gone anywhere in a while, and Denny's one of my best friends, you know that. Besides, her boyfriend just dumped her, and she needs a change of scene." She gave a little snort of laughter that didn't sound amused. "Denny and I have a lot in common."

Jake felt his chest tighten with some inner turbulence. "Wish I could go to the beach," he said sullenly.

"I know you like the beach. Maybe you and I could go for a couple of days after you get home, right before school starts. Maybe take Stephen with us."

"That's weeks and weeks from now," he complained.

"Well, I can't help that," she said testily. Then, in a gentler voice, "I'm sorry, Jake. Sorry we can't work things out the way you want. But I totally love you, and I can't wait for you to get back home."

"Yeah," he said in a neutral voice. Her words had made him feel only a little better, and he was too old to say "I love you" to his mom on the phone, with his father listening. There was nothing else he could say.

One-word answers.

They talked another minute or two, then hung up. She hadn't asked to speak to Jake's father, and he hadn't asked to speak to her.

10

The next morning Jake lay on his back on the lumpy couch, stared for a minute or two at a book, then put it down. He felt restless, but it might be too early to go see Allie or Adrian—it wasn't yet ten o'clock, and both of them usually slept late.

He would have liked to talk to his father about baseball. They'd watched a Yankees game together the night before, and that had been fun, but just this morning in the newspaper he'd read about the Padres playing the Cardinals in San Diego. The score was tied when they went to bed, but according to the paper the final three innings had been amazing. A rookie on the Padres had hit two home runs, and two players, one on each team, had gotten injured, possibly changing the course of the whole season.

This was a game that had to be talked about. But Dad was working, and he wouldn't like being interrupted. Jake sighed. Boring, boring, boring. What was he supposed to do around here?

At that moment he heard a car pull up out front and a

horn beep. It couldn't be for him—it must be someone looking for Allie, or maybe Roger. But he got up and looked out the window anyway. An old white car was nosed in right at his front steps, and waving to him from behind the wheel was Adrian.

"Holy—!" Jake ran outside. "What the heck are you doing?" he said as Adrian sat there with a cocky grin, apparently enjoying Jake's stunned expression. "Whose car is this, your dad's?"

Adrian just jerked his head toward the seat beside him. "Let's roll."

There was a second's pause while Jake's mind registered that of course Adrian didn't have a driver's license, that he had undoubtedly taken the car without permission, and that Chris Berry would hit the roof if Jake so much as *thought* about going for a ride with a boy too young for a license.

Then he walked around to the passenger side and got in.

He felt electric. He felt reckless and wild. He stared at the dusty black dashboard, the cracked gray vinyl of the seats, as if he'd never seen such things. The black steering wheel with Adrian's hands on it was a thing of power and wonder.

Automatically he reached for the seat belt, then dropped his hand. Adrian wasn't wearing one, and neither would he.

The car lurched forward, and moments later they were out on the highway, flying down the slope toward town.

"How'd you get the car?" Jake called over the noise of the wind.

"Miranda went to Rochester with her boyfriend half an hour ago. She left me her keys."

"She left you her keys?" Jake said skeptically.

"Well, not exactly," Adrian grinned. "But she left them where anybody could find them."

"I thought it was your dad's car."

"It is, but Miranda drives it a lot. She has her own keys."

"How'd you learn how to drive?" Jake asked enviously, watching Adrian shift gears with only a little jerking.

"Michael showed me. In his mom's car."

As a huge truck hurtled toward them in the other lane and whizzed past, Jake's stomach fluttered nervously and he thought that he really should put on his seat belt. But he didn't.

Then they were entering town, and the speed limit went down to thirty, though a glance at the speedometer showed Jake they were still going almost fifty, until a red light and stationary cars ahead of them forced Adrian to slow down and stop.

"Where are we going?"

"You'll see."

"Did Miranda tell you she wouldn't drive you anywhere for a month?" Jake asked as the light turned green and the car moved forward again.

"Yeah. She gets all pissed off because I don't take orders from her. But as you can see"—Adrian grinned at Jake, then had to swerve a little to get back in the lane—"I don't *need* Miranda."

They were on a strip—block after block of Kmart, Burger King, McDonald's, Target, Barnes & Noble, Wendy's. Abruptly, without a turn signal, Adrian pulled into a huge parking lot in front of a Home Depot.

"What do you want at Home Depot?" Jake asked as Adrian eased the car into a space between two SUVs. It wasn't his idea of a place to go for fun.

"A vital component of future missions," Adrian said mysteriously.

Half irritated, half admiring Adrian's smug control, Jake resorted to a mock salute. "Whatever you say, captain."

They strolled to the entrance and through the automatic doors like they owned the place. It was huge, with a high ceiling and aisle after aisle of shelving and screwdrivers, washing machines and bathtubs, chain saws and lightbulbs. They wandered wordlessly for several minutes. Adrian appeared to be looking for something, but Jake wasn't going to ask what and give him the satisfaction of not answering again.

Finally, in the hardware section, Adrian saw what he wanted. He walked up to a man standing behind a counter and said, "I need a copy of this, please." He had Miranda's keys in his hand, three keys on a ring with a green plastic frog, and he was removing the car key.

The Home Depot man was white-haired, with creases around his mouth and eyes, and he wore glasses with a horizontal line across the middle. He didn't look particularly friendly as he took the key from Adrian and studied it a moment, then studied Adrian's face. "This your car key?" His dry tone was faintly skeptical.

Adrian smiled disarmingly. "It's my dad's. He's over there." He waved vaguely toward his left. The store was busy, and there were at least three men browsing among the doorknobs and screws and hinges who could possibly have been Adrian's father. "He's always losing his keys," Adrian went on, "so he wants to have an extra."

Even as Jake marveled at his friend's coolness, it occurred to him that Adrian should have said the keys were his mother's; how many men would carry a key ring with a bright green frog on it? But the frog was already back in Adrian's pocket, and if the Home Depot man had noticed, he made no comment. He nodded, picked out a blank key from a rack, and fitted the blank and Adrian's key into a machine, which did its loud grinding work in only a minute.

Back in the car, Adrian shoved the new key into the ignition. "Now we're going to test this baby." The car started up without so much as a stutter.

As he backed out, Adrian said, "Hey, you got any money?"

"No."

Adrian gave a disappointed grunt and then, as he pulled out onto the main road, said, "Well, let's go see who's around."

They drove for ten minutes or so, away from the strip and through residential areas. The houses grew fancier, the yards larger, the streets winding. Adrian drove slowly and didn't seem entirely sure of his way.

"There," he said at last, turning into a long driveway that led to a brick house with tall white columns in front. "This is Marshall's house. He's a guy I know from school."

A new-looking Volvo sat in the open garage, the space beside it empty. Adrian parked in the driveway, and Jake followed him to the door, hanging back while Adrian pushed the doorbell.

It was a warm, clear, blue-sky day. A lawn mower buzzed a couple of houses away, and a sleek black car passed at a leisurely pace. Birds called in the shrubs around the house and in the massive old oaks and maples that lined the street. Jake felt they'd traveled a world away from Tracktown.

A woman came to the door, a tall, slim woman with chin-length dark hair. "Yes?" she said in a cold, polite voice. It was clear she didn't recognize either of them.

"Hi," Adrian smiled. "I'm looking for Marshall. I'm a friend of his from school."

"Oh," she said, seeming to relax a little. "He's not here, I'm afraid. He's away at soccer camp this week."

"Oh, okay. Would you just tell him Adrian Greene stopped by?"

"I'll tell him." She smiled faintly, closing the door.

Back in the car, they were almost at the end of the driveway when a police car cruised slowly by. Adrian hit the brakes a little too hard, and Jake's stomach clenched, but the policeman never glanced their way. Adrian gave him a few seconds to get farther down the road, then pulled out in the opposite direction.

"Okay, let's go find Otis and Flavin. They're always around," he said.

This time they drove to a neighborhood of old frame houses and two long, low apartment buildings that Adrian called "the projects." Michael Otis lived a couple of blocks past the projects in a house with faded green shingles; one side of the front porch was covered with a thorny, climbing bush bursting with hundreds of pink roses.

As Jake and Adrian stepped onto the porch, a little girl peered at them through a window screen, then turned away. "Michael!" she yelled. "You got visitors!"

Adrian sat on the porch rail and lit a cigarette while they waited.

"Greene-man!" Michael stepped out onto the porch. "What you doing here?"

"Just taking a ride," Adrian said coolly, smoking.

"Ride?" Michael looked to the street. "You got the car? Sweet!"

Adrian permitted himself a slight smile. "It was easy. Miranda took off and left her key." He paused to take a puff. "Got it copied just now, so I'll have my own."

"Congratulations, man. Welcome to the world of wheels."

Michael rocked from his heels to his toes, back and forth. He looked at Jake, who was leaning against a post. "Hey, little Jake. You brave enough to ride with this guy?"

Jake threw out his chest in mock outrage and marched up to Michael, who towered nearly a foot above him. "Who you calling little, punk?"

"Who you calling punk, punk?" They shoved and wrestled for the five or six seconds it took Michael to get Jake down. Then they both stood up, panting and grinning, Jake rubbing his neck.

"Wanna go somewhere?" Adrian asked.

"Naah," Michael answered. "Me and Flavin are playing Madden on the Xbox."

"Not anymore," said Ben Flavin, appearing behind the screen door. "You lost, Otis—56 to 6."

"I told you to pause it, you—" Michael's fist took a swing that stopped just short of the door; Flavin ducked despite the screen between them.

"Cheater," Michael muttered. He turned to Adrian. "Okay, let's go somewhere."

They piled in, Michael in the front, Jake and Flavin in the back. While Adrian lit a cigarette, Michael put on his seat belt, and Adrian said, "What are you scared of?"

"I ain't seen whether you can really drive yet. I want my head to stay on this side of the windshield."

Flavin laughed but made no move to buckle his own belt. Jake put on his, rather self-consciously.

But as soon as they were moving he felt great again, electric, exhilarated. Hanging around with these older boys, talking about anything they felt like, on the road in a borrowed car, not a license among them—he'd never felt so free, so far beyond the reach of parents and teachers and principals and anyone who'd tell him what to do.

Adrian drove up a ramp onto the highway—or maybe it was a different highway, Jake wasn't sure—and as they picked up speed a hot wind racketed around in the car, muddying their voices and making them squint. They shot past other cars, past shopping centers and muffler shops and car dealers and a lumberyard, till the buildings thinned out and fields took over, and the car sailed on, sleek and unstoppable. They could drive to California, Jake thought—just drive and drive and drive.

But after a while Jake's exhilaration began to fade, and as though they all felt somewhat the same, the talk slowed and died out. Silence held for a few minutes, and Jake began to feel that the countryside was boring, the road before them dull and endless. He watched Adrian blow smoke out the window. The sun was dead overhead, its brassy light glaring relentlessly off signs and cars. Jake wondered where Adrian planned to go, or if he was just driving. He sort of needed to pee.

After a few more minutes Flavin broke the silence. "Where are we going?" he asked, as though the question had just occurred to him. "I'm hungry," he added.

"Me too," Michael said.

"Got any money?" asked Adrian.

"No," said Michael and Flavin simultaneously.

"Well, why the hell not?" Adrian muttered, slowing down and pulling off to the side of the road.

"Didn't know we were going on a flipping three-day journey," Michael said.

Adrian brought the car almost to a stop on the dusty shoulder, then whipped it around in a U-turn. The motion slung Jake against the car door, the seat belt catching hard at his shoulder. Then he straightened up and watched as the road melted away beneath them.

The mood in the car shifted immediately, and they were all talking again, as though they'd been awakened by the U-turn, or by the sense that they had a destination after all. They talked about who'd make it to the World Series, about Xbox versus PlayStation, about a girl at school who'd gone to Japan for the whole summer.

Houses and stores and churches gathered around the highway; the fields filled up. Then they were flying down a long downhill stretch like a toboggan chute, all the way into town.

They dropped off Michael and Flavin at Michael's house. Jake moved up to the front seat, and with a jolt they pulled away from the curb.

They passed the housing projects, rows of dull red brick buildings, where adults sat on tiny concrete porches and kids played in the grass or on a dusty playground with swings and seesaws. Adrian had to hit the brakes as a boy on a bike darted across the street; he was too slow on the clutch and the car stalled, forcing him to start it again. "Stupid kid," he muttered.

They drove through streets lined with old frame houses, past a small grocery store, an elementary school, a block where the houses had been turned into dentist's and doctor's offices. The sun was beating down, and the people on the sidewalks moved slowly.

Jake hadn't asked where Adrian was taking them, but he wasn't sorry when he finally recognized that they were turning onto the highway toward Tracktown. He was getting hungry, and he really needed to pee now.

"You got any good food at your house?" Adrian asked, accelerating up the ramp.

"Yeah, I think so. Sandwich stuff, like turkey and ham."

"Let's go eat, then."

Jake noticed that Adrian wasn't asking, he was telling. But he didn't really mind.

Adrian swerved across the highway—no turn signal—onto Tracktown's street.

"Hey, park at your house," Jake said urgently. "My dad'll have a fit if we drive up."

Adrian shrugged and stopped the car abruptly in front of his house. As the boys got out, Jake thought he saw a curtain move in a second-floor window. "I think somebody's home," he said, alarmed. "I saw something up in that window."

Adrian glanced quickly at the house, but all the curtains were now still and the windows blank. "Probably just my dad. Miranda can't be back yet."

They started down the potholed street. No one seemed to be around except a couple of seagulls pecking at something in the weeds beside the train tracks.

"What if your dad saw us? Won't he, like, kill you?"

"Naah. If he saw us he'll forget all about it. He's got some really crucial experiments going on right now, so all he thinks about is his work."

"Sounds just like my dad," Jake said, with a touch of bitterness. He wondered if Adrian ever longed for more of *his* father's attention, and he almost asked. He felt something rise in his throat, something that wanted to say how he felt, and find out if his friend felt the same.

But maybe Adrian—fourteen, two whole years older than Jake—was too grown up, too tough to feel that way.

Jake didn't ask.

They were polishing off huge sandwiches—ham, Swiss cheese, lettuce, mustard, pickles—when Jake's father came downstairs.

"Hello, gentlemen," he said, with an air of cheerful satisfaction. "I've done a fine morning's work, finished the most important chapter in my book, and I'm almost ready for a swim. How about you two?"

"Sure," said Adrian. "Could we go to Clipper's Point?"

"Indeed we could. Best place to swim on the whole lake." He opened the refrigerator. "But first I need a sandwich. If you two seagulls left anything edible."

"We left you a few crumbs," Jake said.

They talked about the Padres and the Cardinals while everyone finished eating. Then Jake's father said he'd be ready to go to Clipper's Point in fifteen minutes. Adrian went home to change, and Jake went upstairs.

He put on his swim trunks and sank into the beanbag chair, then slipped on his headphones and put in an Eminem CD. Neither of his parents liked Eminem—too much bad language—but he'd bought the disc with his own money, after all. His mother frowned every time she saw it, but didn't take it away. His father probably didn't know he had it. Jake sat there feeling the beat, the drive, the streetwise rap penetrating his bones.

At Clipper's Point, Chris Berry swam laps while Jake and Adrian played, diving and racing and splashing. Jake kept his guard up, but Adrian didn't pull any aggressive moves, physically at least. He just seemed especially full of himself. He'd yell, "Watch this!" and leap off the dock, goggle-eyed, legs bicycling in the air, as if he was some cartoon character who'd walked off a cliff. Then he'd tell Jake that *his* stunts were "pathetic."

Jake was getting annoyed, but the sky was too bright, the water too deliciously cold, to let Adrian spoil the day.

They came across Peter Glass, crouched on the shore, looking for fossils. He stood up and held out his hand, squinting earnestly at them, freckles standing out against his pale face. "Gastropods," he said. "See, kind of like snails? They're all over the place." He glanced down at the two small fossils in his hand and sighed. "I have a lot of them already. I was just hoping to find a big one that's perfect."

"Snails, huh? Oh wow," said Adrian with a touch of mockery. He glanced at Jake as if wanting him to share the joke.

Jake grinned back, but then said, "Let me see," picking a stone out of Peter's hand to take a closer look.

Peter brightened at this sign of interest, and began explaining rapidly. "These are maybe three hundred million years old. That's how long ago this creature was alive. You can find fossils all around here, but the best place is up the lake about fifteen miles, outside of Wellsville. My mom takes me sometimes. I found my best trilobite there."

"Cool," said Jake, turning over the gray rock in his fingers, feeling the indented shape of the snail-like creature.

"You can come over and see my collection sometime," Peter offered.

"Yeah, okay." Jake thought that might be kind of fun, although he hoped Peter wouldn't launch into a long lecture about everything in the collection.

"Come on, let's swim," Adrian said to Jake.

"Okay."

As they turned toward the water, Peter said, "Hey, Adrian. And—what's your name?"

"Jake Berry."

"Oh. Do you guys want to play with Shamu?"

"Who's Shamu?" Jake and Adrian said at the same time.

Peter pointed toward the grassy area, where an inflated plastic whale, longer than any of them and twice as wide, lay on a towel.

Their eyes lit up, and all three of them ran over to the whale. Adrian grabbed it while Peter placed his fossils carefully on the towel, and a moment later they were all tussling in the water, riding on Shamu, knocking each other off, hooting and hollering.

When Jake's dad swam over to tell them he was ready to go, they begged for more time.

"I guess I can lie in the sun for half an hour," he said. "But next time I call you, we're going. Got it?"

"Okay," Jake said, and hurled himself into Shamu, sending Peter spluttering into the water.

Half an hour later, still wet, Jake and Adrian got into the hot car. After dropping off Adrian, Jake and his father went home and changed, then picked up a pizza for dinner.

It had been a good day, Jake thought as he and his father sat in the kitchen munching on white garlic pizza. The swim had felt great.

And the ride with Adrian—well, it probably wasn't a safe

thing to do. And Adrian was breaking the law, driving without a license. But Jake remembered the thrill of being on their own, beyond the rules.

Jake's parents would be horrified if they knew. But the thing was, they didn't know. It was his secret, his and Adrian's.

CHAPTER

11

That night Allie's boat drifted through Jake's dreams. Adrian was driving and Jake was sitting in the bow; Allie wasn't there. He felt the wind in his face as they powered out into open water, and he felt happy and excited. For a moment there was no Adrian, just Jake and the boat, and the two of them formed one creature, sleek and playful as a dolphin.

The boat bounced over little waves, then coasted smoothly up to a white-sand beach. It was the "Riviera," but this time Jake owned it; he had every right to swim there. He and Adrian were swimming together, but a storm gathered, and they got back into the boat and left. They were going fast out into open water, the sky darkening.

Then Jake looked back and Adrian had disappeared. No one was driving, and terror overwhelmed him. He didn't know how to drive the boat—it would crash—where was Adrian? He woke up trembling. The clock said 2:09. Soon he fell back into an uneasy sleep, and when the four o'clock train roared by, it was almost welcome. He slept a little better after its passing.

Around mid-morning he went out to the dock. The day was warm and humid, the water calm, a fishy smell in the air. He glanced over at Allie's boat. It was a much more ordinary craft than it had seemed in the dream, he thought, looking at its dulled paint and the cracks in the seat boards. There was nothing scary about it. But the good part of the dream, that feeling of flying over the waves—that had been real enough, the same feeling he'd had in the real boat ride, with Allie at the tiller.

As if his thoughts had summoned her, Allie appeared at her back door. She walked out to the end of her own dock and called across to him, "Hey, Jake."

"Hey, Allie cat."

"I don't have Maddy today. I thought maybe you and me and Adrian could take the boat up to a good swimming place and hang out."

"Cool! Let's do it," Jake said.

"Go ask Adrian, okay? I'll pack some lunch for us."

They cruised for miles up the opposite side of the lake, so far that Adrian said, "Do you really know where you're going? I mean, can't we just drop anchor and swim anywhere?"

"We have an anchor, but we don't have two hundred feet of rope," Allie answered. "That's how deep it is out here. And I don't want to move in close to people's houses."

"You really think there's a park up here somewhere?" Jake asked. He too was getting impatient in the hot sun.

"I know there is. Petronius State Park. Just hang on a little longer."

Another ten minutes and it all came into view—a swimming area with a lifeguard stand perched on a floating dock, a huge lawn with picnic tables under tall trees, a playground, a pavilion.

"Great," Jake said. "Let's park this yacht somewhere and jump in."

"Not here," Allie said. "It's really shallow, and it's full of little screaming kids. I know a better place to swim."

"Yeah, but how much farther?" Adrian groaned. "I'm hot. I want to swim."

"It's worth being hot for five more minutes—you'll see," Allie replied.

Jake watched longingly as they left the swimming area behind. They passed a marina where dozens of sailboats and motorboats rocked gently on the wake radiating from Allie's boat. Then there was a small stretch of woods, and the shore curved inward, forming a cove.

Allie pointed them toward the shore, shut off the motor, and let the boat coast to land. There wasn't much of a beach here—the trees came down almost to the water—but it was beautiful, with the trees' reflections turning the water deep green, and it was quiet. Only a few other people were swimming in the cove, adults who had kayaks pulled up on the rocky shore. A sign, posted at the tree line, read SWIM AT YOUR OWN RISK.

The water was glorious. They lolled in it, they floated, they dived and swam deep, they splashed each other and raced the length of the cove. Allie was a stronger swimmer than Jake would have expected, and even Adrian had to make a serious effort to pass her.

Dripping, they perched on a log and ate the sandwiches and cookies Allie had brought. They were quiet, eating and resting, listening to the sounds of seagulls and the droning of motorboats far out in the center of the lake. Faint cries from the swimming area occasionally reached their ears. The kayakers had paddled away, and Allie, Jake, and Adrian had the cove to themselves.

As soon as Adrian finished eating, he lit a cigarette.

"Gross," Allie said, frowning at him.

"You're calling my cigarette gross?" he replied with cheerful mock amazement.

She popped open a can of orange soda. "Yes, because it *is* gross." She appealed to Jake. "Isn't it gross, Jake?"

With Allie to back him up, he realized, it was easy to say what he really thought. "I hate to agree with her," he said to Adrian, "but it *is* kind of disgusting."

Ignoring Adrian's glare, which might or might not have been a joke, he turned to Allie. "Pass me a root beer, would you?"

Allie and Adrian bickered until the cigarette had burned down almost to the filter.

She waved a hand in front of her face. "You're polluting my air. Put that crap away."

Suddenly Adrian smiled. "Okay," he said, and ground out the cigarette with a rock. "I'm done now anyway."

Allie looked at Jake and rolled her eyes.

The center of the lake was crisscrossed by larger and faster boats, so on the way back Allie kept her boat close to shore. They puttered along, the warm breeze not quite banishing the oily smell of the motor.

"Hey, Allie," Adrian said suddenly. "Want to know what I did yesterday?"

"What?"

"Went for a little drive."

"That's exciting," she said mildly. Jake couldn't tell if she was being sarcastic or not.

"In Miranda's car." Adrian paused for a second. "Without Miranda."

Her glance shifted instantly from the shore to Adrian's face. "You mean you drove Miranda's car?"

"You got it," he said coolly.

"You lie a lot, Adrian."

"Ask Jake. He went with me."

She looked at Jake, and he nodded. "It's true."

"Why?" she asked.

Adrian grinned. "For fun. For practice. For getting the hell out of Tracktown."

Several kayaks were moving around a dock ahead of them, and Allie eased the boat farther into open water, away from the kayaks.

"Where did you go?"

"Just driving around. We picked up Otis and Flavin."

Allie looked at him severely. "Do you know how much trouble you could get in for driving without a license? You could get arrested, Adrian. You could probably get sent to a—a detention place, or reform school or something."

Jake was listening uncomfortably, thinking how right she was, and yet how cool it had been to cruise around with Adrian behind the wheel.

Adrian shrugged. "I didn't get caught, did I?"

"Lucky for you," Allie said.

CHAPTER

12

After the 9:30 train had roared its way through Track-town the next day, Jake sat up in bed to see, between the half-opened curtains, rain coming down by the bucketful. Ugh. He'd heard Dad say there was a drought, and he remembered there'd been hardly any rain the whole time since he'd arrived, but still—rain got in the way of almost everything that was fun to do around here.

He went downstairs and sat in the booth in the kitchen, reading the sports pages in the newspaper while his father made coffee.

"Hey, Randy Johnson had a no-hitter," he said.

"I saw that," his father said, coming over to sit down across from Jake. "Best night he's had all season."

For once his father didn't seem to be in a huge hurry to get to work. The two of them sat and talked sports and glanced through the rest of the newspaper, Dad sipping coffee from one of Sam Weesner's fat green mugs.

After a while Jake went to the back door and looked out. The rain hadn't let up in the least—it was hammering on the weathered docks and the rocky shore, plopping like a million gray stones from the gray sky into the gray, seething lake. Something about it made him feel, unexpectedly, a little sad. What was he doing in this place, and where were his friends, his real friends?

He went back to the booth. "Dad?" he said hesitantly.

"Yes?" his father said, folding up the front section of the paper.

"What are you going to do today?"

"Climb Mount Everest. Visit the pope. Maybe sing some opera at Carnegie Hall," his father said with a perfectly straight face.

"Ha-ha-ha, you're so funny. Not," Jake said.

"Well," said his father, getting up, "I'm going to do what I always do—get to work."

"Couldn't you take a day off? Take me somewhere? To the mall or something?"

His father was shaking his head even before Jake finished speaking. "I really have a lot to do, Jake. If I don't keep at it, I'll get behind."

"I'll play chess if you want to," Jake offered, almost pleading. He really didn't want his father to go upstairs and leave him alone, sealed inside this dull house by the relentless rain. His heart was beating fast. Why did this matter so much? he asked himself; why was it such a big deal? It just *was*—he had no other answer.

Somehow, for once, his father seemed to understand, at

least partly. He leaned against the refrigerator for a moment, studying Jake, and then he said, "Tell you what. I'll knock off early today. Give me . . ."—he glanced up at the clock—"till noon and then we'll go get subs for lunch and figure out what else to do. How's that?"

"Cool," Jake said, his spirits lifting. His father went upstairs to work, and he decided to see if Adrian could hang out in the meantime. He found the phone book in the living room, but none of the Greenes in it had a Tracktown address. Well, he'd just have to get wet.

A few minutes later he was splashing down the street toward Adrian's house, water already soaking through the shoulders and hood of his sweatshirt. He rang the doorbell and waited, still getting wet as the wind blew the rain in under the small awning.

No one came. Yet he thought he'd heard voices inside, though it was hard to be sure, with the noise of cars on the highway and water streaming from holes in the gutter onto the ground nearby.

He rang again, and again he thought he heard talking. He remembered that there was a screened porch at the back of the house; maybe they were out there and didn't hear the doorbell. He started off around the side of the house, keeping close to the wall. He'd almost reached the back when suddenly, right over his head, a voice came loud and clear.

"You can't, you can't do it!" It was Adrian, and his voice had a high, almost hysterical note Jake had never heard in it before. He froze, his left side in the rain and his right side sheltered by the house.

"You bet your butt I can." That was Miranda.

"But I can't—you're taking the car—how are we supposed to get food?"

"Chill out, Adrian," she said impatiently. "I'll come by sometimes and bring you stuff."

There were sounds of drawers opening and closing, the scrape of a zipper.

"Come on, Miranda." Adrian seemed to get hold of himself, to put on a calmer, smoother, more persuasive voice. "You don't want to live with him. Sometimes he acts like a real jerk. You deserve better than that."

The answer came back quietly, simply. "Sure, sometimes he's a jerk. But he loves me."

In the face of this steady reply Adrian seemed to panic again; he spoke very fast, his voice rising. "What about him, what about *him*?"

He sounded *afraid*, Jake thought wonderingly. He'd never imagined Adrian afraid of anything. At the same moment Jake realized guiltily that he was eavesdropping—but he didn't want to leave, he was consumed with curiosity. Who was *him*? Did that mean the guy Miranda was going to live with? Or Adrian's father? Or someone else?

But just then Adrian and Miranda moved away from the open window above Jake's head, and all he could hear were snatches: "not mine" . . . "leaving me with" . . . "had enough."

Then he heard the front door open, and he was suddenly terrified that one of them would look around the corner and see him and know he'd been eavesdropping. He darted toward the backyard next door, and as he dashed through the mud and sodden grass he heard Adrian's voice, vibrating with rage: "You rotten bitch!"

Jake ran through two more backyards before coming out to the street. As he glanced back toward Adrian's house he saw Miranda's old white car pulling out, the backseat piled to the roof with bags and boxes. Gravel spun out from under the rear tires as she sped toward the highway, hardly slowing at the edge of it before she pulled out and disappeared, taillights blurring in the rain.

Slowly Jake walked the rest of the way home. The rain had eased up, from a downpour to a steady patter, but Jake hardly noticed. Why was Adrian so upset about his stepsister moving out? Why did he seem so frightened?

Dad took him to a pizza-and-sub place for lunch. They ordered subs at the counter, then sat at a table by a window, on metal chairs with red vinyl seats. The place was on a busy street, and they watched the traffic through a curtain of rain sliding down the glass.

Jake looked around. The restaurant was almost full, and there was a cheerful hum of talking and laughing, over which a fat man behind the counter boomed out the names of people whose orders were ready. Some of those people wore business suits, but most looked more like the two guys with the insignia of a cable TV company on their shirt pockets, or the men who had come in from two phone-company cherry pickers parked across the street.

It was nice, Dad taking him to this place. He wanted things like this to happen more often, and he thought maybe he should act really mature, maybe talk to Dad the way Adrian did.

"Did you start a new chapter on your book?" he asked.

"I did indeed. I've moved on from Roosevelt's first term to his second."

"Berry!" called the man behind the counter, and Chris Berry motioned with his head for Jake to get the food. In a minute he was back with long sandwiches wrapped in white paper, and the two of them dug in.

"So, what did you do while I was working?"

Jake took his time answering, first getting through a big mouthful of hot chicken Parmesan sub. It gave him time to think about whether he wanted to tell Dad what had happened. He decided he did want to tell, but carefully.

"I went over to Adrian's to see if he wanted to hang out, and Miranda was moving out."

"Really? Moving to where?"

"To live with her boyfriend, I think. Adrian seemed really mad about it. He was yelling at her when she drove off."

"Hmm. I wonder if it was a sudden decision."

"Maybe. Yeah, it sounded like it. Like she was kind of fed up and wanted to get out."

"Could be." His father shrugged and took a sip of his soda. "She's an adult—a lot of people her age would get tired of living with a father and a little brother. Maybe she and the boyfriend want to get married."

"Yeah." Jake chewed in silence for a minute. "But you know what's weird?"

"What?"

"Adrian wasn't just mad. He was *scared*. I mean, he really sounded like her leaving scared the heck out of him."

His father looked more serious, and finished a bite of his sub before he said thoughtfully, "So that leaves no one at home except Adrian and his father?"

Jake nodded.

"What's the father like?"

"I don't know. I've never even seen him."

"Never seen him?" Chris Berry's thick eyebrows shot up. "In all the time you've spent hanging around with Adrian?"

"We never go in his house," Jake explained. "We play basketball outside, or hang out at our place, or Allie's house."

"You've never been inside his house? Not once?"

"No."

"Wow," said his father softly. "I wonder what he's hiding."

After lunch they splashed out to the car, then drove to the mall through the still-pounding rain. They spent some time browsing in a bookstore, finally buying two books for each of them. At an athletic store, Jake pressed for new sneakers, but

Dad examined the ones he was wearing and said they were fine. By the time they left the mall, though, Jake had new flip-flops, a new rap CD, and a new T-shirt. Then they stopped for groceries, and when they got home it was past three o'clock and the rain had stopped.

A little later, Adrian knocked on the door. "Let's go play some football," he said. "Otis and Flavin are gonna meet us at the park."

Jake looked at the sky. It was still cloudy, but it did look as though the rain was finished. "Sure. I just have to get my shoes on." He told his father where they were going, and then they were off, past Roger's house and along the rocky, muddy bank, with the highway and train tracks on one side and the lake on the other.

The rain had cooled the day only a little. The sun came out as they walked, and the wet ground steamed. They gagged and held their noses as they passed a dead fish.

Adrian seemed perfectly normal, and Jake wondered for a moment if he'd imagined the note of terror in Adrian's voice that morning. But he knew that wasn't his imagination. He wanted to ask how Adrian was doing, or what was going on with Miranda, but couldn't think of a way to do it without giving away the fact that he'd eavesdropped outside their window.

Adrian talked a lot on the way to the park, but none of it was about what had happened at his house. It was all about baseball, or football, or the Jet Ski he wanted.

They were hot and sweaty by the time they reached the park, and only the faintest breeze moved in from the lake. They found Michael Otis and Ben Flavin in an open field beside the park road, and the four of them quickly agreed on the rules. Because Jake was the smallest, he was paired with Michael, the tallest and most athletic of the boys. It was tackle, but the defense had to count to six by Mississippis before they could rush the quarterback. Once touched by the defense, the QB could run; otherwise, he had to pass to his receiver, who was guarded by the other defense man. Once every four downs, the defense was allowed to blitz—to rush the quarterback without a count.

Thanks mainly to Michael, the Jake-and-Michael team was soon ahead by two touchdowns. Michael was usually quarterback, and he was great at timing a pass. Jake caught most of them, though Adrian or Flavin could bring him down fast.

The game moved quickly. No huddles, just play after play, with Michael occasionally muttering an instruction to Jake, and everyone shoving and panting and sweating.

Sometimes it was Jake who played quarterback, but if he couldn't get off a pass quickly enough, he was easy for the others to flatten. On defense, he gamely tackled Adrian and Flavin again and again, but often he only managed to slow them down. In the instant's pause before each play, when he faced Flavin across the scrimmage line, Flavin grinned and growled and made comically ferocious faces at him. Jake laughed, but nervously.

The goal lines were marked only by a single tree at one end and a car parked beside the road on the other end, so every time one side claimed a touchdown, the other side argued. The arguments were loud, full of swearing and allegations of cheating and lying, but they never lasted more than a minute or two, because all four boys just wanted to get on with the game. Jake was getting pushed around some because of his size, but he wasn't bothered by it much; he felt tough, and proud that he could compete with bigger guys.

The losers, though, were beginning to get irritated, and both were swearing more than usual. Now, when they faced off across the line, there were no more comical faces—Adrian and Flavin just looked grim and determined.

Adrian slapped the ball to start the play, and Jake, as rusher, yelled out the counts. Meanwhile, Michael was all over Flavin without laying a finger on him, his superior height between QB and receiver. No matter how Flavin tried to evade him, Michael was faster as well as taller.

On "six Mississippi" Jake dashed toward Adrian. Ball raised in one hand, the older boy hesitated for a fateful second, as though hoping for Flavin to get free. Jake took a flying leap and caught Adrian off balance; to Jake's amazement, the other boy crumpled under him. He'd sacked the quarterback.

Jake leaped to his feet and did a victory dance, hooting and hollering. Flavin groaned, Michael cheered, and Adrian didn't make a sound. Jake raised his face to the sky and flung his arms wide, and then something hit his back and shoulders like a freight train. His knees hit the ground hard, and one of them struck a rock, sending out shock waves of pain. Something, somebody, was right on top of him, slamming his face into the grass and punching the side of his head again and again.

For a moment Jake was too stunned to act. Then he began to fight back, blocking Adrian's fist with his arm, shoving his elbow into whatever part of Adrian it could reach, bucking and struggling against the weight on his back. He couldn't throw Adrian off, could only stop a few of the punches.

He heard Flavin and Michael shouting, heard Adrian muttering unbelievably foul curses in a voice vibrating with rage. Jake's ears were ringing with the punches, his face burning, his breath ragged, the weight compressing his lungs.

Then the weight lifted, and he rolled up onto his knees, trembling fists raised. Michael and Flavin had pulled Adrian off. He could breathe.

He kneeled there, gasping, staring at his attacker. Flavin and Michael each had one of Adrian's arms pinned.

"What's the matter with you, Greene?" Flavin said, amazement written all over his broad face.

"Yeah, chill out, man," Michael said.

Adrian was still struggling against their grasp and staring murderously at Jake. "That little creep better stay off me or I'll punch his lights out."

Jake's voice came out angry but a little shaky. "All I did was tackle you! We're playing football, remember?"

"Yeah, I saw it," Michael said. "Jake nailed you, Adrian. You just can't believe he did it."

"You're full of—" Adrian stopped. He clamped his mouth shut and stopped struggling. There was silence for a moment, everyone staring at Adrian, whose face was rigid except for a twitching around his mouth, as though he was keeping a lid on some wild thing that wanted to come out.

Then he shrugged off the other boys' grip, and they let him go. "I'm out of here," he muttered. He turned and strode off toward the end of the park, toward Tracktown.

The others watched him go. The back of his faded red T-shirt bore a dark patch of sweat in the center, like a map of some foreign country. Seeing it reminded Jake of the heat of the day, which he now felt surrounding him like a wool blanket. He was still breathing raggedly, as though there wasn't enough oxygen in the humid air.

"That was weird," said Flavin. "Never seen him lose it like that."

Michael picked up the football and spun it between his fingers. "Me either. But he was pretty wired the whole game. All jumpy."

Jake stood up slowly, sending more pain radiating out from his knee.

"You okay?" Michael asked him.

"Yeah, I guess so." In fact he didn't feel okay at all. His knee and his right ear and cheek hurt. His mouth felt swollen and he could taste blood. And he still felt half stunned: his friend had attacked him.

But the way he really felt didn't seem to register with Michael or Flavin.

"Well, let's get going," Michael said to Flavin. "See you later, Jake."

"Yeah, so long," Flavin said, and the two of them headed for their bikes, which lay in the grass nearby.

"See you," Jake said. He watched them get on their bikes and ride away, and then he made his feet move toward Tracktown.

It was only when he neared the end of the park that he realized he was going to have to walk through that long rocky stretch along the lake, that empty strip between lake and highway. He was going to have to walk through there alone, and for all he knew, Adrian might be waiting for him, to beat him up again.

The thought was like a cold fist around his heart, but he tried to reassure himself. Adrian had calmed down, he told himself. And anyway, he could hold his own against Adrian, if he wasn't taken by surprise and attacked from the back. Besides, there was no other way to get home.

The glare off the lake made his head hurt worse. He stumbled on rocks, again and again, and every step hurt his knee.

Just an hour or two ago he'd come this way to the park with Adrian, the two of them talking and joking like friends. The way seemed infinitely longer now.

He kept peering ahead. Luckily, there were hardly any rocks or trees on the whole stretch that were big enough for anyone to hide behind. He saw no one until he reached Track-town, stumbling gratefully onto the paved street. And there he saw only Roger, sitting on his front steps, talking on a cell phone with his long legs stretched out in front of him. His little beard waggled when he talked.

Roger waved to Jake as he kept on talking, and Jake waved back wearily. In a moment he was up the steps, through the holey screen door, and safe inside.

CHAPTER
13

The train at 4:00 A.M. shook him like a familiar night-mare; the roaring and the house quaking scared him every time, but at least now some corner of his mind faith-fully reminded him that it was only the train and soon it would be gone. On this particular morning his mind also reg-istered the soreness of his body, but he was so tired that he sank quickly back into a murky, troubled sleep. If his father got up as usual, Jake didn't hear him.

He woke again to the first faint rumblings of the 9:30 train approaching. His room was awash in light, and he lay on his back with the ends of the pillow pressed up around his ears, comfortably muffled until the train had passed. Then he sat up slowly, his right knee throbbing as he bent it, putting his feet on the floor. There was a tenderness around his right temple and cheekbone, and his left shoulder was sore—he'd probably wrenched it, he thought, when he was trying to get Adrian off his back.

His body hurt more than it had on the walk home from the park, but then he'd been shocked emotionally as well.

Now the shock had faded, leaving a sludge of anger and a puzzled, lingering fog of betrayal. What was Adrian's problem? What had Jake ever done to him?

He went to the bathroom, and when he came out his father was at the top of the stairs, heading for his desk with a cup of coffee. He smiled at Jake. "Recovered from those battles on the gridiron?"

"Kind of," Jake answered. "My knee still hurts."

"Well, it's a good day to rest and read a book, then." He went on into his room, saying over his shoulder, "I'll be in here, in the salt mines."

Jake got dressed and went down the creaky stairs. His father had no idea how appropriate the word *battles* was, because Jake hadn't told him about Adrian's attack—he'd said only that he'd played football with Adrian and a couple of his friends, and had gotten some bruises when he was tackled. Jake wasn't quite sure why he hadn't told his father the whole story—after all, he hadn't done anything wrong. Yet somehow he felt that this was between him and Adrian, and even though Adrian had betrayed him, there still remained a trace of an alliance between them.

He ate some Cheerios at the kitchen table, then went to the couch and picked up the book he was reading. He sat with it open on his lap for a few minutes but didn't feel like reading. His mind kept returning to the crazy way Adrian had turned on him. Suddenly he wished he could talk to someone about this; he almost wished he had told his father everything. But now, of course, Dad was working, and Jake thought he shouldn't interrupt.

And Mom? She would be at work by now, and she couldn't talk on the phone for more than a minute there. Or was she still at the Jersey shore? He couldn't remember what day she was coming back, and even if he could find the number she'd given him, he didn't want to call some hotel and ask for her. He wasn't sure she'd understand this guy stuff anyway. She might just tell him to stay away from Adrian, and that wouldn't help at all.

Then, suddenly, he knew who was the right person to talk to—Allie. She knew Adrian, had gone to school with him, and anyway there was just something about her calm voice, her warm smile, her way of taking him seriously. He walked to the back door and looked out, but her yard and dock were empty. Then he returned to the front of the house and stepped outside. It was warm but not yet hot, and there were puddles in potholes and beside the road from yesterday's rain, glinting in the sun. There was no one on the street, or on Allie's front porch, and little sound except from the highway. If Allie was there, she wasn't playing the piano.

"Hey," he said when she opened the main door, the screen still between them. She wore a red sleeveless top, and her hair was pulled back in a ponytail.

"Hi, what's up?"

"Um, I was just wondering if maybe I could borrow a couple of CDs? Like, I'm getting really bored of the ones I have."

"Sure, come and hang out for a while if you want to." She pushed the screen door open for him.

"I'll bring them back, okay? I won't lose them or anything."

"I'm not worried," she said, leading the way into her living room. "I know where to find you."

The living room was bigger than Sam Weesner's, but the furniture looked about the same—old and lumpy. Loose, flowery slipcovers were draped over the couch and two armchairs. The braided rug was fully occupied by Maddy, a large dollhouse, and a scattering of toys.

"Hi, boy," Maddy said, looking up from a doll she was struggling to dress in a jacket and pants.

"Hi, Maddy." Jake grinned at her. "I have a name, did you know that?"

"Yeah, but I don't like it."

"You don't like my name?" he said, making a face of exaggerated astonishment, eyes and mouth wide open. He was hoping to make her giggle, but she didn't.

"No. It's a bad boy's name."

"What do you mean, it's a bad boy's name?" Jake laughed. "I'm not a bad boy."

But she was frowning down at the doll, tugging a sleeve over its plastic hand, and didn't answer.

"There was a boy in her preschool named Jake," Allie explained, "and he was always hitting the other kids."

She led him over to a bookcase with a CD player and speakers on top. The shelves were full of discs, and Jake was secretly relieved to see that they weren't all classical. In fact, there was a little of practically everything there—Frank Sinatra and the Beatles, Beethoven piano sonatas and *Greatest Hits of the Fifties*, the Rolling Stones and Patsy Cline, U2 and Miles Davis, Eminem and Mozart.

"Wow, you must like just about every kind of music there is," he said, crouching down for a closer look at the disks.

"Well, I like a lot of different music, but these aren't all mine. Some of this stuff is Wendy's, and some of it's my mom and dad's."

She sat down beside him on the floor, folding her legs yoga-style. He noticed again how long her legs were, below her weathered blue-jean shorts.

She ran her fingers lightly over the disc cases, then pulled one out and showed it to him. "Ever hear this?" It was *Solo Piano*, by someone named Philip Glass. Jake shook his head, and she stood up and put the disk in the player. A strange melody, different from anything he'd ever heard, filled the room. It was peaceful music, a little sad—and that quick impression was all he had time to take in before Maddy interrupted.

"I don't like that!" she shouted. "Turn it off!"

"In a minute, Maddy, okay?" Allie answered. "I just want Jake to hear a little of it."

"No!" said Maddy, standing beside the dollhouse with her hands on her hips. "I want Tom Knight. I want 'Alligator Jump.'"

"Shhh," Allie said sternly. "Or go to your room."

Maddy gave the dollhouse a furtive kick, but she quieted down. Jake tried to listen to the music, but he was distracted by the sight of Allie, who was sitting on the floor again, eyes closed and hands on her knees. As far as he could tell, she'd instantly become entranced by the sound. Her face was turned toward it, her whole body leaning slightly in that direction, as if spring had just arrived and she was drinking in the first warm sun.

Jake closed his own eyes and concentrated, trying to hear what she heard. The melody was complicated, not easy and catchy like a rock song; you thought it was one thing for a moment and then it kept sliding into something else. Sometimes there were a few notes in isolation, like slow, fat raindrops at the start of a downpour. The music seemed to be about mysteries that no one was ever going to explain.

For a minute he felt all of that, but then his mind drifted away, and he opened his eyes. When the piece ended, Allie opened her eyes too, and reached up to push the power button. "What did you think?" she asked Jake. "Did you like it?"

"Yeah, kind of." He wished he could think of something

smarter to say, or that he could honestly say he loved it. "I mean, it's kind of mysterious."

She lay back on the floor, knees in the air, staring at the ceiling. "Mysterious and beautiful. It's just so, so beautiful. I could listen to it for hours."

If you say so, Jake thought. He began looking through the discs, taking out a few that he might want to borrow. He picked out U2, Tupac, *Sgt. Pepper's Lonely Hearts Club Band.*

Allie sat up with a sigh. "Hey," she said suddenly. "What happened to your face?"

"Oh." He touched the bruised place self-consciously. For a few minutes he'd forgotten all about the incident he'd wanted to tell her about. "I was playing football yesterday."

"Did you get hit with the ball?"

"No, I got hit with Adrian's fist."

"Adrian's fist?" She stared. "You got in a fight with Adrian?"

"No, I got jumped by Adrian and he tried to beat the crap out of me," Jake said bitterly. He told her the whole story. "I thought he was my friend, you know?" he added. "But he's just insane. He ought to be locked up."

"Wow, he really flipped out," Allie said. "Like, out of control."

"Yeah, and you know what? That's not the first time. When we were swimming once, he just about drowned me. He was holding me down under the water."

"Are you serious?" she said, mouth open in amazement. "What did he do that for? Was he mad at you?"

"No way, it was totally out of the blue. Then he said he was only fooling around. Just kidding. Like, ha-ha."

"Weird," Allie said.

"I just don't get it," Jake said, with an impatient shake of his head. "Why would he do something like that to a friend?"

"I don't know," she said thoughtfully. She pulled the red elastic band out of her gleaming brown hair and smoothed it back, replacing the band. "He's always had a temper—I've seen him get mad at people at school. He's not the relaxed, easygoing type, you know? But I've never seen him completely flip out like that."

Jake shrugged. "I've seen about all I want to see of it." He turned his attention to the CDs again, pulling out a Green Day album that Stephen had told him was really good.

"I just wonder," Allie said slowly, "if Adrian's acting this way because of his family somehow. There's got to be something weird about his father—nobody ever sees him. And his sister—well, I don't—"

"Oh—Miranda!" Jake interrupted. "I totally forgot about the other thing that happened yesterday, before the game."

"What?" Allie demanded. Jake launched into the story of his visit to Adrian's house in the rain, and all he'd heard and seen as Miranda moved out.

"He sounded *scared*?" Allie said when Jake had finished.

"Yeah. It doesn't make any sense, but I know that's what I heard."

"Sounds like he's afraid to be left there with just his father. Maybe his father is really mean or something."

"I don't think so," Jake shook his head. "Adrian talks about him sometimes, and he never says anything like that."

"Have you ever seen bruises on Adrian, like somebody's been hitting him?" Allie asked quietly.

Jake thought for a second. "No, have you?"

She shook her head, and they sat in silence for a moment. Jake was thinking about the awful idea of a grown-up beating up a kid, and also about how ridiculous it was to imagine a tough, cocky boy like Adrian letting anybody beat him up.

"Still," Allie said slowly, "it's got to mean something—his stepsister takes off, and he's so upset about it that he sounds scared, and he's yelling at her in the street, and then the very same day he flips out and attacks you."

Then another idea seemed to strike her. "Remember when you told me Adrian never let you come in his house? Is that still true?"

"Yeah, I've been hanging around with him all summer and he's never once invited me in," Jake said, tapping his fingernails rapidly on the CD case he was holding. "I told my dad about that and he thought it was really strange. He said, 'Wonder what he's hiding.'"

"Exactly," said Allie, suddenly folding her arms with a determined look. "He's hiding something. And it's about time somebody asked him what it is."

Jake raised his eyebrows. "Don't look at me. I'm not asking Adrian anything. I'm staying away from him."

Allie frowned. "Well, I'll ask him then." She was fiddling with the ends of her ponytail, and looked worried. "But maybe it's better not to ask straight out—he'd probably just lie and say everything's fine."

"He would, definitely," Jake nodded emphatically. All he'd wanted was to talk about the incident at the football game; he'd never envisioned this conversation taking a turn toward how to save Adrian from whatever his problem was. The whole thing was a little alarming.

"But, Jake," Allie said, still looking worried, "we're Adrian's only real friends."

"Huh?"

"Of course we are. He's only lived here six months or so. I've never seen any of the kids from school coming to Tracktown to hang around with him."

"What about Otis and Flavin?"

"Oh, them," she said dismissively. "They're not real friends; they're just guys he plays football with now and then. They're kind of jerks, anyway."

They said nothing for a moment, Jake looking through the discs again.

Finally Allie said, "I just have a feeling Adrian needs help."

"I just have a feeling Adrian's a psycho," Jake retorted. "And I'm staying out of his way."

An hour later he went home with a handful of discs. It

was great to have different music to listen to for a while, he thought as he sat on the couch, putting a disc in his CD player. And it had felt good to tell Allie about Adrian's attack, and to hear what she thought about it.

Maybe she was right that Miranda's departure had spooked Adrian somehow, that he was afraid of being left alone with his father. But why? What was wrong with Adrian's father?

14

For the next couple of days Jake didn't see Adrian at all. He spent part of each morning hanging around the backyard and dock, talking to Allie and Maddy or skipping stones. The lake was deep azure under a sky of sun and a few thin clouds, and then, both afternoons, darker clouds rolled in like army tanks and unleashed brief but dramatic thunderstorms.

Jake watched from the window of his father's room as lightning danced over the lake, now gray-green and metallic. A thunderstorm over a big lake was an entirely different thing from the storms he'd seen back in Wendell. The lake, which always changed its hue as the sky changed, now became an arena for the storm's performance, the houses and hills around it rising like viewing stands. Thunder boomed across the surface, each sizzle of lightning met its reflection, and the clouds poured out rain like endless bolts of dully shimmering fabric that rippled down and down and dissolved themselves in the all-absorbing lake.

Without Adrian, and with rain keeping him inside in the

afternoons, Jake began to notice his father talking on the phone a lot. There were two phones in the house, one in the living room and one in his father's bedroom, and neither one was portable. His father didn't even own a cell phone; he hated them, said he didn't want phone calls intruding all the time.

Once Jake woke up around midnight and heard his father talking in his bedroom. Instantly wide awake, Jake was wild with curiosity, but his own bedroom door was closed, and it had a loud and extremely reliable squeak—he didn't dare open it to eavesdrop. He lay utterly still on his bed for a few minutes, but all he could hear was an occasional murmur without a single understandable word.

On the next afternoon, as the storm clouds were rumbling slowly away, Jake was in the kitchen getting a snack when he heard the phone ring. Dad was upstairs, and just a second before, Jake had heard him go into the bathroom and shut the door.

So he went into the living room and picked up the phone. There was a second's hesitation on the other end, and then a woman's voice said, "May I speak to Chris, please?"

"He's not here," Jake answered. He didn't know why he lied, and he was astonished at how swiftly and fluidly the lie came out. It was as though some powerful instinct had taken him over.

"Oh." She sounded surprised. "Do you know when he'll be back?"

"No."

"Okay, I'll try later."

As Jake hung up, his father called from the top of the stairs, "Was that the phone I heard?"

"Yeah, but it was a wrong number."

Another easy lie. Jake returned to the kitchen and resumed making himself a peanut butter sandwich.

In the late afternoon Jake felt restless. He wanted to do something, but certainly not with Adrian, and he didn't feel like going to see Allie. Finally he decided to see if Peter Glass was home. Peter would probably want to show him his collections, and then maybe they could think of something else to do.

The street was wet and puddled, but at least the air felt clearer and less humid since the thunderstorm. There were glimmers of sun at the edge of a mass of clouds, and everything—cars, houses, the weeds along the tracks—looked freshly washed.

Peter's grandpa sat, as usual, in his green-webbed, aluminum lawn chair on the porch. He was reading a book, but looked up as Jake approached. He was an average-size man, but something about his sharp nose made Jake think of an elf. His white hair was combed straight back, and his keen blue eyes examined Jake's face with an expression that seemed friendly yet serious.

"Hi," Jake said from the bottom of the steps. "I'm looking for Peter."

The old man was slow to answer. "I've seen you playing basketball with the Greene boy," he said at last.

Jake nodded.

"And what's your name?"

"Jake Berry."

The old man just continued to search his face.

"Is Peter home?" Jake asked. He was starting to feel uncomfortable as well as impatient.

Only then did the old man smile slightly. He stood up and shouted through the screen door, "Peter! You have a visitor."

When Peter came to the door, his rather dull, square-jawed face lit up. Jake had a feeling he was lonely, and that by showing up like this, Jake had somehow made his day.

"Hi," Jake said. "I thought maybe, if you're not doing anything, you could show me your fossils and stuff."

"Sure," Peter said eagerly. "They're up in my room—come on up."

Peter's room contained a closet and a wide, blue-painted dresser, but there was little evidence that he ever put away his clothes. Shirts, shorts, boxers, and socks, along with books and pencils and birthday cards and coins and candy wrappers, littered the floor and the unmade bed. This place was even messier than Jake's room.

But one thing here was absolutely, startlingly neat—the bookcase. The bottom two shelves were ordinary, each perhaps a foot high, mostly filled with books. Above that, though, were at least a dozen shelves only a few inches apart, and each held a neat array of shallow cardboard boxes, all carefully labeled.

"Those are my collections," Peter said unnecessarily. He sounded both proud and nervous. Jake went over and began reading the labels: BUTTERFLIES, MOTHS, AMMONITES, TRILO-BITES, BIVALVES, GASTROPODS. He pulled out the box labeled AMMONITES and found a dozen or so smaller boxes within it, each containing a fossil, nestled in a bit of tissue paper, and a tiny card with a date and place written on it. Most of the fossils had a spiral shape, and some of them resembled snail shells.

Jake put the box back and pulled out the one labeled TRI-LOBITES. These turned out to be weird little buglike creatures, bumpy gray shapes emerging from gray rocks.

"Those are really common around here," Peter said, looking over Jake's shoulder. He pointed to one of the larger fossils. "That's my best one. See how it's got three sections? That's why it's called a *tri*-lobite."

Jake poked a finger at another one. "Looks kind of like a sow bug—you know, those roly-poly bugs."

"No, it doesn't." Peter looked from the fossils to Jake, apparently both amazed and disappointed. "It doesn't look *at all* like a sow bug. Look—head, thorax, tail. Also there are three sections lengthwise too. Sow bugs don't have anything like that."

This was getting way too serious for Jake. "I used to *be* a sow bug, in my previous life," he answered. "That's why I see them everywhere."

Peter looked at him weirdly for a second, then laughed.

"In my next life I think I'll be . . ." Jake slid the trilobites back onto their shelf and waved a hand along the shelf above it, settling finally on the butterfly box. "I'll be one of these dudes here. I'll be something *pretty*."

This box had a glass lid, pressing the butterflies against a bed of white cotton. "I caught these myself," Peter said, "except for that one. I bought that." He pointed to a spectacular cobalt-blue specimen. "Those live in Brazil."

"Wow," Jake said. It was the largest butterfly he'd ever seen, and the brilliant blue of its wings seemed almost artificial.

"I don't have many butterflies yet," Peter said. "I just got into butterflies and moths a couple of months ago."

"They're cool," Jake said, admiring two black-and-yellow swallowtails. He'd seen them lots of times but hadn't known their name until he saw it neatly printed on a tiny card between the two specimens. Peter showed him his long-handled net and his killing jar, an old mayonnaise jar that he said contained a chemical to kill the butterflies quickly.

"Cool," Jake said again. He really had liked seeing Peter's collections, but now he felt like getting out. "Want to go outside for a while?"

The doorbell rang as they were going down the stairs.

As soon as they got to the bottom, they could see Adrian, standing just outside the screen door with a basketball under his arm.

Jake felt something cold clutch at his chest and stomach. He hung back as Peter went to the door.

"Peter, what's up?" Adrian said.

"Oh, nothing. Just showing Jake my collections." Peter half turned, as if to show Adrian who was behind him, and Jake moved slowly toward the door. Peter's grandpa had disappeared; there was only Adrian on the porch.

"Hi, Jake," Adrian said matter-of-factly. He was looking not at Jake but at the basketball, which he was now trying to twirl on the tip of his index finger.

"Hi," grunted Jake. He packed a lot of hostility into that one syllable.

"Came over to see if you guys wanted to play some basketball."

Jake wondered if Adrian had known he was here, or if he'd been willing to settle for Peter's limited skills.

Peter muttered a vague "Ah, I don't know."

"No thanks," Jake said flatly.

Adrian stopped spinning the ball and held it in front of his Rockets jersey. The usual cocky expression on his thin face seemed to be undermined by a touch of anxiety. "Oh, come on, it'll be fun. You two against me."

"What, so you can jump me again?" Jake said in a hard voice.

"Hey, I meant to tell you, sorry about that." Adrian licked his lips nervously. "I just got kind of . . . worked up."

Peter was looking curiously from one of them to the other. Jake said nothing at first, just looked at Adrian. He thought he saw a genuine, deep worry in Adrian's eyes, and he had a feeling that Adrian actually cared what he thought, cared about what Jake's answer would be.

Besides, Jake did want to get outside, out of Peter's house, and he did long for the feel of that ball in his hands, the swish through the net.

"So, okay, let's play," he shrugged.

"Cool," Adrian replied, thumping the ball a few times.

But Peter, clearly disappointed, muttered, "Think I'll stay here."

"No, come on," Jake said. "I need help against him."

"I stink at basketball," Peter said, staring at his bare feet, the wall beside him, anywhere except at the two taller boys.

"That's okay. You'll get better. Anyway, together we'd have to be better than me by myself."

Privately, Jake suspected that might not be true, and his suspicion turned out to be right. A pass to Peter often fumbled its way into a turnover; a shot by Peter usually meant no basket, just a rebound for Adrian. Jake winced with frustration whenever this sort of thing happened. All the same, it felt good to play, good to test himself against Adrian's skills. And he knew he wouldn't have liked himself much if he'd gone off with Adrian and left Peter behind.

Finally, as the sun was getting low over the hills on the far side of the lake, Peter's mother came out to their front porch and called him home for dinner. Jake and Adrian played for a few more minutes, and then Jake called time. "I need a break," he said, panting.

"I'll get us some water." Adrian disappeared into the house. As before, he closed the main door as well as the screen door behind him on his way in, and again on his way out with glasses of ice water.

They sat on Adrian's front steps, gulping down the water, watching the traffic rushing down the highway toward town. The air was motionless, and so were the weeds along the train tracks—the blue, daisylike chicory; tall goldenrod; spreading sweet pea. Jake knew a few of these flowering weeds because his mother had always liked them. Sometimes in the summer she would stop her car on the side of a road and gather up armfuls of them to bring home.

Adrian lit a cigarette, took a deep drag on it, and then silently held it out to Jake. Startled, Jake said, "Oh—uh, no thanks."

"Come on, just take a hit. You never tried it, right?"

What harm could it do to take a few puffs? Jake took the cigarette and put it between his lips. He drew in a breath and instantly pulled out the cigarette, coughing.

"Ugh." He handed it back to Adrian. He thought the cigarette was disgusting, though he wasn't sure whether that meant he was smart or just that he was a kid compared to Adrian.

Adrian didn't laugh at him. "You get used to it," he said. "Then it tastes really good." But he didn't press Jake to take another hit.

Jake finished his water, then said, "Well, I'd better get going. My dad probably has dinner ready."

"Okay." Adrian put his glass down on the step. "I'll walk over with you."

"Cool," said Jake. He hadn't forgotten the football game—no way—but Adrian was great to hang around with when he was acting normal, and Jake was glad he was coming over again.

But they hadn't gone more than a few steps before a white car turned in from the highway, and both boys paused to watch. The car came directly toward them, and Miranda was behind the wheel.

"Let's get out of here," Adrian muttered, grinding out his cigarette on the pavement. But the car had stopped in front of his house and Miranda was calling him.

"Hey, Adrian, I brought groceries. Come on, help me carry them in."

"I'm going to Jake's" was the sullen answer.

She got out of the car and stood with her hands on her hips. "You ungrateful pig—I brought you groceries so you wouldn't have to go on the bus. At least you could carry the bags."

"Oh, all right, all right."

Miranda opened the trunk. There were three brown paper bags inside, all very full. As she handed one to Adrian, Jake offered, "I'll take one." This, he thought, would be a chance to see the inside of Adrian's house, maybe even get a glimpse of his mysterious father.

But Adrian quickly grabbed another bag. "We've got it. Just wait here for a second, okay?"

Miranda picked up the third bag. "Shut the trunk for me, Jake, wouldja?"

The two of them went inside, this time without closing the solid door. Jake slammed the trunk and stood there, occasionally catching the sounds of voices and cabinet doors closing.

As they emerged from the house, Miranda was saying, "Well, make him cash his check. He always did it before."

"That was because you took him in the car," Adrian said, almost desperately. He was keeping his voice low, but Jake heard him nevertheless. "He's not going to get on a bus. I can't *make* him."

Miranda blew out an exasperated breath, and didn't bother to keep her voice down. "You two can't do a damn thing by yourselves, can you?" She had reached the car and stopped, fingering her gold necklaces and shaking her head.

"Well, you took the car," Adrian snapped. "I could drive it if it was here."

"You can't drive a car, you little punk."

"Wanna bet?"

"Well, you ain't driving this one." She got in the car and slammed the door. For a second she just sat there, staring at the dashboard. Then she pushed back her dark hair and looked at Adrian. "Okay, look, I'll come back tomorrow and take him, all right?" She started the motor. "I'll be here about noon."

The car jerked into reverse, turned around, and headed out to the highway.

Quickly, as if to forestall questions, Adrian said, "You gotta go home, right?"

"Yeah."

"Hang on a second."

Jake watched him light another cigarette, and then they started down the street, Adrian launching into a description of last night's Cardinals-Braves game. As much as Jake loved baseball, at the moment it wasn't what he was curious about.

15

After that, Adrian was practically living with Jake and his dad, except that he didn't sleep there. He'd show up soon after the 9:30 A.M. train and they'd hang around, playing catch or basketball, or sometimes Magic, with Jake's box full of cards. Or they'd go over to see Allie, and if she didn't have Maddy they might take the boat up to the state park and swim.

In the afternoons, Jake's father sometimes took Adrian, Jake, and Allie swimming at Clipper's Point. Sometimes Adrian borrowed books from Jake's dad, and they'd talk about them over dinner. Often, after dinner, the three of them would watch baseball.

But why was it always at Jake's house? Adrian had a TV, bigger than the midget thing that Jake and his father had. Jake had never seen it, of course, but Adrian had told him it was three times the size of theirs. It would be so much better to watch the games on a bigger screen, and anyway Jake would have liked to get away from his house and his father now and then. But Adrian never invited him over, and Jake grew more and more irritated.

One evening in the living room, when Adrian glanced at his watch and said, "Almost time for the game," Jake decided it was time to say something.

"So," he said casually, tucking some of his baseball cards back into their box, "how about we watch over at your house for a change?"

Adrian looked momentarily startled, then shook his head regretfully. "My dad doesn't like for me to have people over—sorry. He just has all these delicate experiments going on, you know . . ." His voice trailed off.

Jake noticed that his father had stopped in the middle of putting away old newspapers and was watching them both intently.

"Well," Jake said, "it's not like I'd be messing with his stuff or anything."

"I know," Adrian said. "But he's just so picky about things like that. Says he has to concentrate. It's an absolute rule—nobody can come over when he has experiments going."

As if you care about grown-ups' rules, Jake thought.

Adrian looked at Jake for a moment. Jake knew his expression was disgruntled and annoyed, and he didn't care if Adrian saw it. Getting up from the couch, Adrian stretched, not altogether convincingly, and said, "Actually, I'm pretty tired. I think I'll just go home and chill. I probably won't even watch the game."

Jake shrugged. "Okay, see you later."

When the door had closed behind Adrian, Jake burst out, "What's the matter with him? He's got a better TV than we do, and he just hangs around here all the time and won't let anybody else come to his house to watch. What a jerk."

"He doesn't want you to meet his father." Chris Berry put the newspapers in a bag, then glanced up at Jake. "There must be something strange about him, so Adrian is ashamed of him."

"Well, maybe," Jake said slowly. But he still felt irritated. "I'm going outside till the game starts," he muttered, and walked quickly through the kitchen and out the back door.

He took long, deep breaths of the cool air outside. It was not yet dark, but there was a softness in the air, a tinge of gray and lavender on the hills across the lake, where the sun had dropped from view. He walked out to the end of the dock and sat down, looking out over the gray-green water.

He wasn't asking for much—he just wanted to see a major-league game on a decent-size TV, and do some of their hanging out at Adrian's house instead of only at his. And Adrian—who was always over at Jake's house, eating their food, going swimming with them, hanging around—wouldn't let him come over even once. Could his father really be that embarrassing?

He heard a door open and turned to see Allie coming toward him.

"Hey, what's up?" She padded onto the dock in her bare feet and sat down beside him.

"What's up is I'm fed up with Adrian," Jake answered grumpily. He told her what had just happened. "My dad says it's because he's ashamed of his father."

"Yeah," Allie said. "I mean, he obviously likes hanging around with you. But he just won't let anybody come in his house."

"Yeah, but so what if his father's a little weird? He could still let a friend come over and watch a game."

Weird. Suddenly Jake remembered the man he'd always called, in his mind, "the scarf man"—the wild-haired man he'd seen when he'd gone out alone at dawn, and again when he and his father were returning from a movie. But now he had an entirely new idea.

"Allie," he said slowly, "have you ever seen a creepy-looking guy hanging around—wears a winter scarf?"

She'd been gazing out at the lake, but now she turned to look at him curiously. "Yeah, two or three times. He's got long gray hair, and he acts kind of sneaky, or maybe scared."

"Exactly," Jake said. "I've seen him twice, and so has my dad. Allie, do you think that's . . ."—the thought was so creepy, he could hardly say it—"Adrian's father?"

She stared at him, her deep brown eyes wide. "I don't know," she said. "But it did cross my mind."

"Why?" he asked urgently. "Why did you think it might be Adrian's father?"

"Well, he was hanging around on the rocks by the lake, just past Adrian's house. And I never saw him before the Greenes moved in."

Jake nodded. "Both times when I saw him, he was down near that end of the street."

She was silent for a moment, then shook her head and said firmly, "We shouldn't jump to conclusions. We haven't seen him coming out of Adrian's house, or sitting on his porch, so who knows? He might not even know the Greenes. He might just be some crazy homeless guy who hangs around the lake to fish."

"But if he *is* Adrian's father . . ." Jake let the sentence trail off.

Allie shivered slightly. "That would explain a lot," she finished.

Two days later, poking around the kitchen cabinets for something for breakfast, Jake glanced at the calendar that hung on the wall and realized it was time to turn the page. It was Saturday, August 1, and that meant he'd be going home in two weeks, or three at the most. The last time he'd talked to his mom, she'd mentioned that, said she couldn't wait to see him, said she'd talk to his dad soon about the best day for her to come and pick him up.

In a way, he was ready to go right now, he thought, lifting

the July page and fitting the little hole over the nail in the wall. He missed his mom, his friends, his own room with all his own things in it.

But in other ways he wasn't quite ready to leave Track-town behind.

He would definitely miss Adrian and Allie. It would have been an incredibly dull summer without them. He felt so free with them, talking and laughing, zooming around in Allie's boat, swimming in the enormous lake. He thought about Al-lie's warm, patient voice, the way she really listened to him, the way she loved the boat and the water.

And Adrian had been great to play sports with and hang around with, except for those bizarre times when he'd turned on Jake. But somehow those incidents didn't cancel out the powerful connection between them. It was more than a love of basketball and baseball and swimming. Jake didn't know quite what it was, but it had something to do with fathers.

And what about his own father? Jake put cereal and milk on the table, trying to think through what a summer with Dad had been like. They'd had a lot of fun sometimes, swim-ming and watching baseball games and going to movies. There'd been only a few times when Dad had been really grouchy and told Jake to leave him alone. So why did he feel this pang of disappointment when he thought about this sum-mer, and the summer coming to an end?

Because I wanted more. The words were as distinct as though some quiet, authoritative voice had spoken them aloud, directly in Jake's ear. He sat down on the high-backed bench in the booth, staring at the milk carton without seeing it.

He'd wanted Dad to make it up to him—make up for leaving him behind, moving away, driving off in the station wagon while Jake stood there blinded by the glare. Make up for not having been there all year, except a few weekends—not seeing his baseball games or helping with homework or talking sports with him. Make up for not even letting him glimpse his other life.

And somehow that hadn't happened. They'd hung out together, watched baseball and gone swimming, and all that had usually felt good, sometimes even great. But his father still had a new life that he wasn't part of, and Jake was still hungry, dissatisfied—as if he'd been starving, and when he finally got a good dinner, he was allowed to eat only half of it.

Jake, Allie, and Adrian sat companionably on Adrian's front steps, drinking big cups of ice water. At first all three of them had fooled around with the basketball, passing and shooting, and then they'd played Horse, which Adrian won easily. Then Allie had dropped out to watch while the boys threw themselves into a fierce game of one-on-one.

Jake could have sworn that Adrian had grown this summer, just in the time they'd known each other—less than two months—while Jake himself, he was sure, hadn't grown at all. He hoped that explained why Adrian kept on beating him.

Adrian was talking about a video game he liked, a combat game with World War II soldiers.

"I know," Jake said. "I have it at home—I mean, at my mom's house. It's a great game."

Allie rolled her eyes. "I will never understand why boys just love to shoot things."

Adrian grinned at her. "Naah, you wouldn't understand." Then he said to Jake, "So why don't you get your dad to put it on his computer? So you could play it whenever he's not working."

"He won't. He says he's already let me put a couple of games on there, and he doesn't want anything else taking up space."

"Why don't you just buy it and install it when he's not around? He'll never notice."

"Oh yeah, right," Jake said, thinking of how angry his father would get.

"My dad would ground me for a week if I did something like that after he'd already said no," Allie said.

Adrian shrugged. "Me, I don't let my old man tell me what to do."

Jake drained the last of his water and chewed on a piece of ice. Then he lightly punched Adrian's arm. "Hey, how come I've never met your old man?"

With another shrug, Adrian looked away. "He's busy, like I told you. He works all the time."

"I want to meet him. Let's go in and see—maybe he's not busy right now."

Allie's eyes met Jake's, and he knew she was going to back him up. "Yeah," she said. "I'd like to meet your dad too."

Adrian glanced swiftly at them, a flicker of alarm crossing his face. "Can't," he grunted, shifting his eyes to the depths of his cup. "He's definitely working now."

"Maybe we could just come in and say hi for a minute," Allie said. "I bet he wouldn't mind that."

"I told you, we can't," Adrian said, his voice rising a little. "We just can't."

But Jake didn't want to take "no" for an answer. He wanted to defy Adrian, who always seemed to be in charge. He wanted to satisfy his curiosity, which spiked every time Adrian dodged the possibility of someone entering his house. And he *liked* Adrian; maybe Allie was right when she said there was something wrong at Adrian's house, something his friends should know about.

"Adrian, buddy," he grinned, "we're going in."

And he jumped up, bounded up three steps, and opened the door to Adrian's house.

16

Hey!" Adrian and Allie were right behind him, and Adrian almost ran into Jake as he stopped short a few feet into the house. They were in a tiny entrance hall, with stairs to the right, and in front of them was the kitchen. Jake had never seen a kitchen in a state like this. Dirty dishes filled the sink and towered above it in precarious stacks. Plastic grocery bags, empty or half full, were scattered across the counter and the floor. Cabinet doors stood half open, revealing a few cans of food, a few cups and plates. The dirt and stains on the vinyl floor were obvious even at this distance.

Against the back wall of the kitchen stood a small table with a fake wood-grain top, with a folding metal chair on each side. And in one of the chairs sat a man Jake had never seen.

He was small, probably no taller than Adrian, and nearly bald, with a few long wisps of brown hair in disarray around his bare crown. He wore glasses with black frames, a plain gray T-shirt, a pair of dirty khaki shorts. His lower legs and feet were bare, and as sickly white as the belly of a fish. He did not appear to be doing anything at all. A magazine lay on the table, but it was closed and upside down. The table held nothing else except a mug and a couple of crumpled paper towels.

The man stared at them with hugely wide eyes, reminding him of a rabbit frozen in the glare of headlights. He said nothing.

Jake was equally frozen, stunned by the weirdness of the scene—the filth everywhere, and the strange silent person in the middle of it. He could hear Adrian, or Allie, breathing rapidly behind him.

It must have been only a few more seconds, though it seemed longer, before the man shifted his gaze to the table-top, then spoke without looking up.

"We're not used to visitors here," he said in an anxious, apologetic voice that was so soft Jake could hardly hear it. He didn't smile, and his hands gripped the edge of the table.

"Oh—um—sorry," Jake said.

At the same time Allie said, "Oh—we're sorry to disturb you."

All three of them stood rigid. Jake wished he'd never come in here, wondered if he should just back out of the room, yet he wanted to know more.

The man plucked nervously at his chin, where he had a few days' beard. "No visitors, Adrian," he said shakily, still without looking up. "No—no visitors."

"Wasn't much I could do about it," Adrian muttered.

The man stood up then, breathing hard, and looked around, wild-eyed—as if he were looking for an escape, but Jake, Allie, and Adrian were standing in the doorway. Then he moved quickly over to a door Jake hadn't seen before and opened it, stepping in so that the door blocked him from sight.

There were no sounds of footsteps. Jake was sure the man was standing still, a few feet away, with the door between them like a shield.

Jake looked at Adrian, who wouldn't meet his gaze. Allie was staring at the door.

With the expression of someone taking vile medicine, Adrian said quietly, "Come on, Dad, that's a closet."

Nothing happened for a moment, and then the man stepped back into view, trembling as he shut the closet door, again glancing wildly around like a trapped animal.

"I better—I better go upstairs," he said desperately, almost panting. He looked at Adrian. "The birds—up there." Then louder, with a sharp note of anxiety: "I want to go see the birds."

"Okay, Dad," Adrian said, and his voice was dry but somehow gentle. "Okay, go see the birds." He pulled Jake by the sleeve to one side, and Allie moved too, leaving the doorway wide open.

With a look of relief, Adrian's father walked quickly past them. They heard his steps on the stairs, then the creaking of floorboards above them.

For a long moment Adrian looked at the chair where his

father had sat. Then he went over to the sink, took a cup from a nearby cabinet, and filled it with water. He took a drink before he spoke, still facing the sink.

"He's not always like this. Sometimes he makes more sense."

"That's—that's your father," Allie said softly.

Adrian turned toward them at last. "Yeah," he said flatly. "That's my father."

Jake looked at the mess everywhere, then back at Adrian. "He doesn't really do experiments, does he." It was more of a statement than a question.

"What do *you* think? He can't even remember what day it is. All he does is watch TV and watch his two little parakeets." Adrian's voice was bitter but carefully controlled.

Allie spoke cautiously. "Has—has he always been like that?"

"No. He used to be just shy and nervous and really quiet. Kind of depressed. He's gotten weirder lately."

"Does he stay in the house all the time?" Jake asked.

"Almost. He gets scared outside. Like the world is too big for him."

"Wow," Allie said softly. "But how do you get money? I mean, he doesn't have a job, does he?"

Adrian put his cup down on the table and sat down wearily in the chair across from the one his father had sat in. "He used to, when I was little. I don't know what it was, exactly, but he went outside somewhere to work. My mom was still with us then. We lived in Buffalo. After she left he still did that job for a couple years, I guess, because that's where he met June—that's Miranda's mom."

"So they got married?" Jake said.

"Yeah, but June was already sick. She was sick all the time. She died when I was nine."

"That's terrible," Allie said. "Did you like her?"

"Yeah, she was nice. But she was always sick, you know. It was some kind of cancer. And she didn't have any other relatives. I think she married my dad because she knew she might die and she wanted Miranda to have a home."

They were silent for a moment. Then Allie said quietly, "So you lost two moms."

Adrian flinched. "June wasn't really like my mom."

"What about your real mom?" Jake asked. "Is she—well, is she really an actress?"

"She might be," Adrian snapped defensively. He looked at his knees, and his voice dulled to a sullen murmur. "She left when I was five. I've never heard from her since then."

Jake felt that hit his heart, and couldn't speak. Allie opened her mouth and closed it, looking ready to cry. Adrian just sat there fidgeting with the cup of water.

Finally Jake asked another question. "Did your dad quit his job after June died?"

"Yeah, or maybe right before that, I'm not sure. He worked at home for two or three years, doing data entry for some company. That was when he started staying in all the time.

All he did was work at the computer or hang around the house with his parakeets and watch TV. I don't think he ever talked to anybody except me and Miranda. And the birds."

Jake leaned against the wall. "You just came here last winter, right?"

"Yeah, in January."

"Why did you move here?" Allie asked.

Adrian hesitated, as if choosing among several ways to answer. "Well, first, my dad lost the data-entry work. I think he was messing up on it. He was starting to act kind of scatterbrained, plus he had a bad back and couldn't sit at a desk all the time. Then he couldn't pay the rent anymore, and we were about to get kicked out of the apartment.

"But Miranda talked to one of the teachers at the high school, and he told her about getting Dad to sign up so he could collect disability money. So finally that came through, and Miranda was working after school and weekends, so we had enough to pay rent."

"But that was still in Buffalo, right?" Jake said.

"Well, around Buffalo. We kept moving farther out, because it was cheaper."

"Did you have to change schools all the time?"

"A few times." He frowned, as if remembering how hard changing schools could be.

"Ugh," said Jake. "We moved when I was in third grade, and I had to go to a new school. It was awful at first."

"Yeah."

What a rotten life, Jake thought. Your mother leaving, your stepmother dying, your father losing his job and acting weird, moving around all the time, never having enough money.

"So, why did you finally move to Tracktown?" Allie asked.

"My great-aunt owned this house. When she died, she left it to my father. All of a sudden we had a free place to live, so we moved here."

"Mrs. Lewinsky was your great-aunt?" Allie said, and Adrian nodded.

They were all silent for a minute. The creaking upstairs had stopped, and all Jake could hear was the sound of traffic through the window, and a buzzing that might have been a motorboat on the lake.

"Well," Adrian said finally, "now you know what I have for a father." He sounded embarrassed as well as bitter, and he wasn't meeting their eyes.

"Actually"—Jake managed a small grin—"he's a lot better than I thought he might be."

Adrian looked up, and there was a touch of relief as well as puzzlement in his lean face. "What do you mean?"

"Well, there's this weird guy I've seen a couple of times, just hanging around at night. A guy with a lot of long, straggly hair, and he wears a scarf like it's winter."

"I've seen him too," Allie put in.

"Yeah, so have I," Adrian said, "but what's that—wait, you thought—?"

"Since nobody ever sees your father," Allie said gently, "we were afraid that might be him. And he looks kind of scary."

"Definitely not my father." Adrian smiled faintly. "Wrong hair."

"Yeah," Jake said. "Wonder who that guy is, though."

"Some hobo jumping trains, maybe."

"Yeah, maybe." Jake heard more footsteps above him, possibly moving toward the stairs, and realized that he had no desire to meet Adrian's father again, even if he was harmless. The man was just too strange.

Allie seemed to have the same thought. "I should probably go home now," she said. She still looked shaken.

"Yeah, me too," Jake said. "Maybe we'll see you tomorrow, okay?"

"Wait." Adrian was following them toward the front door. "Don't tell your parents about this, okay? About my dad and everything. Don't tell anybody."

"Why?" Allie asked, pausing just inside the door.

"Well, he's really not that bad, you know?" Adrian looked anxiously into their faces. "I mean, most of the time he's pretty normal. He just stays inside a lot. It's just once in a while he doesn't make any sense, like the way you saw him."

"Yeah, okay, but what's the big deal if other people know about it?" Jake wondered.

"You guys gotta listen to me," Adrian said desperately, his eyes boring into Jake's, then Allie's. "Some people might think my dad's too—too crazy to have a kid living with him. What if one of your parents starts asking questions? Or somebody calls social services? I could get sent to a foster home or something. Especially since Miranda's not here anymore. *You can't tell anybody.*"

For a moment Jake and Allie stood still, wordless in the face of such desperation. Then Allie flung her arms around Adrian in a brief, hard hug. "We won't. We won't tell anybody."

Jake held out his hand, and Adrian grasped it. "I won't tell," Jake said quietly. "I swear."

17

Late the next morning Jake and Allie went to Adrian's house and knocked. They saw him peer out the front window before coming to the door.

"Hey," he said gruffly.

"Want to hang out?" Jake said.

"Sure. I'll be out in a minute."

"It's wicked hot out here," Allie said. "Can we come in?"

Adrian shook his head immediately, but Allie was ready for that.

"There's nothing to hide from us, Adrian," she said with quiet force. "We're your friends."

He stared at her for a moment, then said, "Well, I guess it would be okay for a little while. My dad's upstairs, so we could stay downstairs."

He led them to the small living room, where they all sat down in the only seats, three battered armchairs. An uneasy silence overtook them. Jake and Allie looked around, taking in a scene nearly as chaotic as the kitchen had been the day before. There was one small table and a bookcase half filled with books; the tops of both were covered with dirty dishes and candy wrappers, some of which had fallen to the floor. Even in the dim light, which entered through and around a thin, sagging curtain in the front window, Jake could see a layer of dust on everything.

Adrian followed their glances. He got up abruptly and put a disc in a CD player that sat on the floor. The music filled up the silence, but still no one seemed to have anything to say.

Finally Adrian said, "What do you guys want to do?"

Jake didn't answer, but what he really wanted to do was leave. This place was depressing, and he kept wondering if Adrian's father was going to come downstairs, and whether he'd freak out somehow when he saw them.

Allie answered slowly. "Well, we kind of just wanted to see how you were doing. And . . ." She brightened suddenly. "I know—we'll help you clean up."

She might as well have suggested they do some ballroom dancing. "Clean up?" Jake and Adrian repeated together in identical, slightly stunned voices.

"Sure," she said, as if that were the most natural thing in the world to do with your friends on a summer day. When they continued to stare blankly, she added, "Well, the place could use some cleaning, right?"

"Well, yeah," Adrian said, "but I don't really care, you know?"

"Yeah," said Jake. "I mean, it's not like my idea of a fun thing to do."

She gave them a severe look. "Come on, guys. Adrian and his dad will feel much better if the place is cleaned up, and with three of us we can do it really fast."

"Naah, forget it, Allie," Adrian advised, leaning back in his chair.

"Good idea," Jake agreed.

She stood up and glared down at them. "Don't be such *boys*," she said witheringly.

She grabbed a few dishes from the table and marched into the kitchen. Jake and Adrian heard water running and dishes clattering, and they looked at each other.

"When did she get so bossy?" Adrian said.

Jake shrugged. After a minute, he said, "I guess we should help her."

"Guess so," Adrian sighed.

It took half an hour for them to gather all the dirty dishes from downstairs—no one suggested checking upstairs—and wash, dry, and put them away.

Allie was still in her commanding mode. "Adrian, get a bag and pick up the trash, okay? I'll wipe off the table. And, Jake, see if there's a broom in that closet, would you?"

A minute later, hearing Adrian's footsteps going upstairs, Jake stopped sweeping.

"What if his father comes down here?" he muttered to Allie.

Her sponge paused on the table, and she looked at him. "He's not going to hurt anybody. I'm sure he's harmless."

"Well, yeah, but . . ."

"I know. He creeps me out too," she admitted.

"Then why were you so hot to come in here and do all this stuff?"

"Because—" she hesitated. "Because nobody wants to be alone with a secret like this. Adrian needs us. He needs for us to know what it's like, living here."

"I guess you're right," Jake said slowly. "It's just—it's all so weird."

Before she could answer, they heard Adrian returning and quickly went back to their tasks.

Jake looked up to see Adrian standing in the doorway, looking agitated, a garbage bag clutched in his hands. "Guys, you better clear out—he's getting really nervous."

"Okay, sure," Jake said with relief. He grabbed a dustpan, hastily swept most of the dirt into it, and dumped it into the garbage bag.

"Are you coming with us?" Allie asked.

"No, I gotta stay here and try to calm him down. I'll see you later," he said, his voice growing more urgent. "Just go, okay?"

That afternoon Jake's dad took all three of them to Clipper's Point. Jake wanted to ask Adrian what was going on with his father, but it was hard to find an opportunity, with so many people around.

They'd been there about an hour when Jake pulled himself up onto the dock and saw that no one else was on it. Adrian and Allie were in the water nearby. He called them over, and they climbed up beside him.

"So, how did it go with your dad? After we left, I mean."

Adrian shook his head. "Not so good. He was kind of upset."

"You mean because we were there?" Allie asked, pulling back her hair and squeezing water out of it.

"Yeah. Like, he was mad at me for letting people in. And he was all upset about things being moved around."

Allie looked puzzled. "But we didn't move anything except dishes and trash."

"I know. It's just—I guess he just doesn't like anything changing."

Allie sighed, and Adrian quickly added, "It was really nice of you to do all that. I mean, it's great to have clean dishes for once."

"Even that much change upsets him?" she said wonderingly. "Just having things cleaned up?"

"Yeah." Adrian stared down into the greenish water. "He was pacing around everywhere downstairs. Kept saying, 'It's not right, it's not right.'"

"Weird," Jake said, then wished he hadn't as Allie frowned at him.

Adrian saw her look. "That's okay. It *is* weird," he said glumly. Then, with a touch of defiance, he added, "But he's not bothering anybody. As long as nobody reports us, we'll be okay."

. . .

That night Adrian ate dinner with Jake and his father, and then they watched baseball on TV. But it wasn't a game that any of them cared much about, and after a while Jake's dad went upstairs to read. Jake and Adrian decided to shoot a few baskets before dark.

They sauntered down the street in the fading light, catching glimpses of pink-and-orange sunset between the houses. They waved to Peter's grandpa, who sat in his usual chair on the porch. He was reading a book, but looked up as they passed and silently lifted his hand.

"Don't old people usually want to sit where they can look at something pretty, like the lake?" Jake said, keeping his voice down. "Why doesn't he sit out back and look at the sunset?"

"Sometimes he does," Adrian replied. "But he's a funny old guy. I think maybe he likes the front because he can see everybody coming and going."

At the next house, the one between Peter's and Adrian's, they saw a man putting a key in the door. He glanced at them and half nodded, then went inside. Neither boy said anything; Jake remembered Adrian telling him that the people in that house were never friendly.

They had to search briefly for the basketball, which had rolled into a patch of weeds along the side of the house. The streetlight came on as they began to play.

Peter came over and stood around with his hands in his

pockets, watching their game. They said nothing to him until the game was over. Then Jake said, "Hi, Peter. Want to shoot a few?"

They messed around, shooting and dribbling, but the darkness grew quickly, and the streetlight wasn't close enough to help much. Jake watched Peter's shot take a hard bounce off the rim and bounce away toward the end of the street. Jake was nearest, so he darted after it. Just as he managed to grab it, he looked up, and a chill went down his spine.

The scarf man was sitting in the darkness twenty feet away, on the slope at the end of the street. He sat with his knees hunched up, and the scarf was wrapped close around his neck. His wild hair lifted slightly in the breeze, and his narrow eyes were watching Jake.

Jake backed away a few steps, then turned and hurried back to Adrian and Peter. "The scarf man," he whispered to them. "Over there."

Adrian took a rapid, nervous look, but when he spoke his voice sounded more irritated than anything else, as if he wanted to hide his fear. "I wish he'd quit hanging around here. Who is he, anyway?"

Jake wasn't expecting anyone to answer the question, but Peter said, "That's Jonah."

The other two stared at him. In all the times Jake had wondered about the scarf man, it had never occurred to him to ask Peter.

"My grandpa told me about him," Peter said in a low voice. He straightened his shoulders, his earnest face glowing as he basked in their attention. "His family lives out in Taylorsville, but he's kind of crazy and he doesn't like to live with them. He was in the war in Vietnam, way back, and his mind got all messed up. He's scared of people, so he hangs around the lake by himself—sleeps in the woods and goes fishing."

"How does your grandpa know all this?" Jake asked.

"Oh, he knows everybody in Taylorsville—he grew up there. Besides, he talked to Jonah once."

Jake took another glance over his shoulder. Jonah hadn't moved.

Adrian looked that way too, then turned back to Peter. "So what's this guy gonna do, pull out a butcher knife and come after us?"

"Grandpa thinks he wouldn't hurt anybody," Peter said.

"Well, he looks like a total lunatic," Jake said.

"Peter," his mother called from the porch. "Time to come in."

"In a minute, Mom," he yelled back.

Jake was watching the scarf man. Was it the loudness of Peter's voice? For some reason, at that moment Jonah stood up quickly and melted into the darkness beyond the pavement's end.

"Right now, Peter," she said in a warning voice.

"Oh, all right," he muttered. "See you guys later." He took off running.

"Anyway, that creep is gone," Jake said. He was still holding the basketball, and realizing how tightly he'd been gripping it, he made his arms relax a little.

"He's like my dad," Adrian said softly, his eyes on the slope at the end of the street. "Only out in the woods instead of in the house."

"Your dad's not that bad," Jake said. "This guy is really scary."

But Adrian didn't seem to hear him. He just stood staring into the darkness where Jonah had gone.

The next morning Adrian came over to Jake's house, and after breakfast they went next door. It was a Wednesday, so Allie was taking care of Maddy. They listened to music and talked for a while, and then Jake and Adrian agreed to play with Maddy so Allie could have time to practice the piano.

They sat on the rug on the living room floor, the sound of Beethoven sonatas filling the house, while Maddy showed them all her toys, telling them the names of the stuffed animals and dolls. She chattered away, and between the loud piano and her little-kid lisp, the boys didn't get half of what she said. But Maddy didn't seem to notice.

When Allie had finished practicing, Jake said, "Let's go shoot some baskets."

She looked at the clock and shook her head. "You guys go. I'd better stay here. Pretty soon I'll have to give Maddy some lunch and get her to take a nap."

Jake and Adrian played hard, sweating under the fierce sun. Adrian won, as usual, but Jake made some tough shots.

"You're getting better," Adrian said, panting after his winning basket, as they stepped into the shade of the house and let the ball roll into a bush.

"Yeah" was all Jake said, but he was pleased that Adrian had noticed. It was true, too—all the practice with Adrian had helped his aim and his ballhandling skills.

Adrian went inside to get water, and Jake waited on the porch. He leaned against the front railing, facing the door, which Adrian had left open. From the kitchen Jake could hear the clatter of ice cubes, but otherwise the house was quiet.

Then he heard a faint creaking of the stairs, and Malcolm Greene—Adrian's father—appeared and turned toward the front door. He was wearing the same shorts and T-shirt as the last time Jake had seen him. His hair was disheveled, and his face was etched with anxiety.

For the briefest second or two they stared at each other, and then Malcolm vanished into the kitchen. Jake felt as if he'd seen a ghost.

He heard water running and an indistinguishable murmur between Adrian and his father. Then the phone rang, startlingly loud, from a table at the far end of the hall. On the third ring Adrian came out of the kitchen and, with a swift glance at Jake, moved to the phone. His hand hovered over it for a moment, hesitating, before he picked it up and said, "Hello."

"He's not here."

"Um, I guess you could try tomorrow."

A longer pause. "Oh. Well, thanks, but he's okay. He doesn't need anything."

"Yeah, I'm his son."

"No." Jake heard alarm in Adrian's voice. "No, you don't need to come by. He's not here a lot, because—because he's got this job, and the hours are sort of, like, irregular."

"Yeah, okay."

"Bye." The last word was faint. When Adrian turned around, his face was white. He walked slowly into the kitchen, then out to the porch with two cups of water.

"What?" Jake said.

"Social services. They might come and check on us."

They sat on the front steps, and Adrian wrapped his arms around his knees.

"Maybe they won't come," Jake said, keeping his voice down. "It's good you said he has a job, so maybe they'll figure they don't need to check on him."

Adrian shook his head anxiously. "I don't know if she believed me, though. I have a feeling she didn't. See, she's called before. Twice. She never said she was social services till today, but it was the same person. I knew she was social services anyway, 'cause who else would be calling my dad? Nobody ever calls him."

They sat in silence for a moment.

"Why are they calling?" Jake asked. "You think somebody told them—well, told them you guys needed help?"

"Somebody must have," Adrian answered broodingly, staring at the ground. "How else would they even know we exist? Some nosy moron must have called them."

"Like who?" Jake asked.

"I don't know. We don't even know a lot of people around here. It'd have to be somebody in Tracktown, unless maybe Miranda blabbed about us to some nosy friend of hers. Or maybe my English teacher last year—I saw her at the grocery store a couple weeks ago and she was asking a lot of questions. I told her everything was fine, though."

After a brief silence, Adrian went on, his voice so low Jake could barely hear him. "I knew this kid once, in Buffalo. His dad wasn't around, and his mom was on drugs and booze all the time. He got taken away from her and put in a foster home. He had to change schools and everything. I saw him at a mall maybe six months later. He said the foster parents hit him all the time."

Jake didn't know what to say. He wished Allie was there—she would know.

Then Adrian looked up, took a breath, seemed to pull himself together. "That won't happen to me, ever. I won't let it," he said fiercely, his eyes burning into Jake's. "I know how to take care of myself. I've got a plan."

"What kind of plan?" Jake said.

But Adrian refused to say more.

They ate lunch at Jake's house but turned down his dad's offer to take them swimming. Then Adrian left to get his Magic cards, saying he'd be right back.

Nearly an hour passed, though, before Adrian returned. Jake was stretched out on the living room rug, sifting through piles of cards.

"What took you so long?" he asked impatiently.

"Miranda's back," Adrian said, dropping a plastic bag full of cards on the floor. "She drove up right when I got there, and she was all mad and upset. Had a fight with her boyfriend."

He sat down beside Jake. "She brought a suitcase, so I guess she's going to stay for a while."

"That's good, isn't it?" Jake said. "I mean, if social services people come, then you've got another grown-up—well, sort of a grown-up anyway."

"Yeah, it's good. I think my dad's glad to see her too. She's usually pretty nice to him, because he took care of her after June died—as much as he could, anyway."

Adrian chose a deck from his bag and set it down in front of him. Then, his face and his tone darkening, he said, "It won't last, though. She's had fights with Lanny before. She'll go right back to him as soon as he apologizes for whatever he did. I give it two days, max."

18

Jake, you think you could stay here by yourself for a night?" Chris Berry asked that evening. Adrian had gone home, and the two of them sat across from each other in the booth in their kitchen.

Jake looked up from his spaghetti and meatballs. "How come?"

"I need to do some more research. And for my field, the best library in this part of the country is at Cornell, in Ithaca. A couple of hours from here. So I thought I'd go over there tomorrow, work for a while, spend the night in a motel, do a little more work the next morning, and then come back."

"I've never been to Ithaca," Jake said. "I could come too."

His father shook his head. "It wouldn't work, Jake. I'd be busy in the library and wouldn't be able to take you places. There'd be nothing for you to do."

"You could drop me off at a mall or something. Or a museum. I could get around by myself," Jake insisted.

But his father was shaking his head long before Jake finished speaking. "On your own, in a strange town? Not a good idea. Maybe I could take you there some other time. But right now I'm pushing to get a chapter wrapped up, and this last bit of research has to get done."

"Aargh," growled Jake, half playfully. He was both disappointed and pleased at the prospect of being left on his own for more than twenty-four hours. Once again he felt shut out by his father and his father's work. But this would also be a chance to do whatever he wanted, without his father telling him what to do. For a day and a half, he'd be as free as Adrian.

Chris Berry drove away around 8:00 A.M., taking his laptop computer and a small suitcase. He'd given Jake the phone number of the motel and a lot of instructions about locking the doors after dark and not using the stove and shutting all the windows if it rained. Jake had rolled his eyes at every word. Then they'd briefly hugged each other, and a minute later the station wagon rumbled out to the highway.

Jake went back inside and flopped onto the couch. For a few minutes he just lay there, listening. He heard the traffic, of course, the endless traffic on the highway, as well as the rise and fade of a motorboat's roar out on the lake. When the traffic noise dimmed for a moment, he could hear the soft notes of a mourning dove, probably perched on the telephone wire, and the vibrant sounds of Allie's piano.

Inside the house, though, nothing made a sound. If his father had been home, he would have been virtually silent anyway, working away on his book. And yet Jake could feel the difference, could feel that he was alone in an empty house.

He picked up the book he'd been reading, read a few pages, and dozed off until the 9:30 train gave Tracktown its usual shake-up. Then he went to the kitchen, yawning, looking forward to a day on his own. No doubt Adrian would show up before too long.

About a half hour later Jake was sitting on the couch again, but the book lay forgotten on the coffee table, and he was staring at the black metal of the woodstove without seeing it. His hands were clenched on his knees, and his blood rushed with emotions he could hardly name.

He didn't even feel like the same person who'd been quietly reading, there on the couch, a few minutes before. Two phone calls had changed everything.

First, out of the blue, a call from his friend Stephen, back in Wendell. Stephen's family was going on a trip, which included three days at his grandmother's house, near a lake just thirty miles from Tracktown. It would only be a little out of their way to stop and pick up Jake, and they could bring him back after the visit. And could he *please* come, because Stephen's grandmother's house was so boring except for the lake, and if Jake didn't come there'd be no one to swim with except his little sister. And if Jake did come, they could play Magic and swim and hang out.

Jake was sky-high with elation. It would be so great to see

Stephen, go somewhere new. He'd have to call Dad to ask, though, because Stephen wanted to pick him up tomorrow around noon, and Dad wouldn't be back that early. He told Stephen he'd call him back.

If only his father didn't hate cell phones so much. But a quick check of the clock in the kitchen told him he might be in luck. By this time Dad should have reached Ithaca, and just maybe he had arrived at the motel but hadn't yet left for the library.

He dialed the motel and asked for Chris Berry. "Room 201," the desk clerk said, and put the call through. Jake was bursting with impatience as the phone rang six times. At last the click of a phone being picked up—but the "hello" was a woman's. For a second Jake was speechless. "Oh," he blurted out. "I was looking for Chris Berry."

She didn't say, "You've got the wrong room." That was what she should have said. That would have been the right answer.

She said, "Just a minute," and then he heard his father's deep "Hello."

Jake couldn't say a word.

"Hello?"

At last he managed a low "Hi."

"Jake? Is that you?"

"Yeah."

"What's up? Is everything okay?" His father sounded nervous.

"Yeah, things are okay," he said slowly. His brain felt numb.

"So . . . there must be some reason you called me."

Jake hardly heard these words. He was still processing the sound of the woman's voice saying "Hello," saying "Just a minute"—an almost familiar voice—the same voice he'd heard once before on the phone, asking for Chris.

"A friend from the college," his father had said a couple of times, when Jake had asked who he'd been talking to.

"Jake?"

"You've got a *girlfriend*." The cold numbness in his brain was starting to wear off, and his heartbeat quickened.

"Yes." A certain wariness in his voice.

"You lied to me." Now the words came faster, and his voice rose. "You said you had to do research, and all you're doing is—is—"

"Jake, listen," his father said sternly. "I did not lie to you. I *am* here to do research. I'm also spending some time with Angela, who teaches in my department. She came here for a conference, and I—"

"I don't care about her stupid conference! What about Mom?"

"Jake, your mother and I have been separated for almost a year. We're not married anymore, not in any real sense."

Jake understood that in a way, knew it was true, but how could he say that, when it felt so false, so wrong? His parents belonged together, or if they couldn't be together, at least they shouldn't be with anyone else.

"So why were you *hiding* your girlfriend?"

"I wasn't—look, why don't we talk about this when I get back tomorrow? That will give you time to calm down. Then we can talk about it as much as you want."

"I don't want to talk about it," Jake muttered sullenly. And he didn't want to think about what his father and this woman might be doing in that motel room.

"Look, Jake," his father said gently. "I know this is hard to take. But we'll talk about it, and it'll be okay." He paused for a moment. "Anyway, why did you call me?"

Jake explained about Stephen's invitation, but all the pleasure had gone out of the plan, and his voice was dull.

"It's okay with me," his father said. "But you don't sound too excited about it. Are you sure you want to go?"

No, he wasn't sure, not anymore. But he didn't want to see his father, he wanted to get away. "Yeah, I'm sure," he answered.

"Okay, then. Pack up some clothes and a toothbrush, and don't forget sunscreen. Get Stephen's grandmother's number and leave it by the phone for me. And I'll see you in a few days, okay?"

Jake called Stephen back, speaking quickly, mechanically, getting off the phone fast. Then he went out to the lake and stood in the shallows, hurling rock after rock as far as he could. Each one, after a launch so hard it wrenched his arm and shoulder muscles, sailed defiantly over that glassy green expanse. But in seconds each one plunged and lost itself in the inescapable fact of the lake.

He didn't know how long he'd been standing there in the hot sun when he heard a door open and close. He didn't even look around. But a moment later Allie was standing beside him. "Trying to fill up the lake again?"

He didn't answer, just kept methodically bending to pick up fist-size rocks and throwing them one by one. Out of the corner of his eye he saw her watching him and knew she was wondering what was wrong. But she stayed silent.

Jake's arm was starting to hurt. He picked up one last rock, then dropped it just beyond his toes. "My father has a girl-friend," he said bitterly to the fast-approaching ripples on the surface. The boat that had made them was hardly more than a speck, far down the lake.

"He told me he was going to do some research at Cornell, but he's just—hanging out with his girlfriend in a motel. The liar."

"How did you find that out?"

Jake explained about Stephen's invitation and what had happened when he'd called the motel.

"What a way to find out," Allie said. "It would have been a lot nicer if he'd just told you about her."

"It'd be a lot nicer if he didn't have a girlfriend."

"Well, he'd have one sooner or later, wouldn't he? I mean, my friend Amber's parents split up last year and her dad's had about six girlfriends already."

"My parents aren't even divorced yet," Jake snapped.

She said nothing to that, just bent over and picked up a small, flat stone, then sent it skimming over the lake. Jake counted mechanically as it skipped six times before sinking.

Both of them skipped stones in silence for a few minutes, and then Allie said, "I think I'll go see if Adrian's home. Want to come?"

"Sure," Jake answered dully. The intensity of his feelings had ebbed, leaving him without any idea what he wanted to do next. Going to Adrian's house seemed as good, or bad, as anything else.

Jake hung back a little as they approached the house, suddenly realizing he wasn't all that eager to see what was going on. Run into Adrian's father again? Run into Miranda, who was always edgy and might still be upset? No thanks.

Allie, though, didn't hesitate for a second. As she went up the steps ahead of him he heard voices from inside, and noticed that for once the main door was wide open behind the screen. This piqued his curiosity enough to propel him to the top of the steps, right behind her.

19

He needs help," Miranda was saying angrily, a few feet inside the door. Adrian stood facing her with clenched fists at his sides. They both looked up and saw Allie and Jake. For a moment, no one said anything.

"Adrian," Allie said, "are you okay?"

"'Course I'm okay," he grunted. "Come in if you want. Maybe you can get her to make sense for a change."

As soon as they stepped inside, Jake could see that Malcolm Greene was in the kitchen. He was leaning against the wall, his eyes closed, as if everything was so exhausting he had to shut it out.

"You're the one who's not making sense," Miranda said. She turned to Jake and Allie. "I've just been trying to talk to Malcolm about getting some help, like seeing a therapist or something. It's not healthy, the way he lives—hiding out in the house, no job, never sees anybody, nothing to do."

You couldn't argue with that, Jake thought.

"Soon as I came back here," Miranda went on, "after being gone for a while, I saw how it was. I got so used to it when I lived here, it almost seemed normal. But then I came back and I thought, this is crazy. It's no way for a person to live. It's bad for Malcolm and it's bad for Adrian too."

"Leave me out of it," Adrian retorted. "And leave him alone too. He doesn't want to go to any therapist."

"Is that what he said?" Jake asked. He felt awkward talking about Mr. Greene as if he weren't there, as if he couldn't hear what they were saying.

"Yeah," Miranda said, more quietly. "But if Adrian would just help, maybe we could talk him into it."

"It wouldn't do him any good," Adrian insisted anxiously. "Besides, once you get those people involved—like social workers and therapists—they start checking out the whole family. They'd be here in no time, nosing around. They'd say there's no adult in charge here, and then they'd dump me in a foster home."

"Well," Allie said, "maybe Miranda could count as the adult. I mean, she's old enough, right?"

"I don't know if they'd go for that," Adrian said.

"Me?" Miranda said. "Give me custody of a thirteen-year-old boy? No way am I ready for that."

"I thought you were fourteen," Jake said.

Adrian shifted his eyes away. "Well, almost."

"Your birthday's in December, runt," Miranda said. "That's not 'almost.'"

"Shut up," he muttered.

"Anyway, I want a life." She tossed her head, dark hair

flying. "When I get enough money, I'm gonna get my own apartment."

"Miranda," Allie said slowly, "did you call social services?"

"No. Adrian already asked me that, and I told him it wasn't me. I have no idea why they've been calling." Her voice took on a note of defiance. "But I say if they want to visit, great, let 'em come. Maybe Malcolm would end up getting some help."

Jake glanced at Adrian and found him staring at Miranda with smoldering eyes. Malcolm Greene was looking at his stepdaughter too, and he looked frightened.

"I'm going—I'm going to bed for a while," Malcolm said shakily. "Don't feel too good." He walked slowly past them and up the stairs.

When the sound of his footsteps ceased, silence lingered, and for a moment no one moved. Then Miranda started to walk away, and Adrian called after her, with a touch of fear in his voice.

"What are you going to do?"

She turned and faced him with a slight shrug. "Nothing, for now. I don't want to force him into anything. I'll try to talk him into it later. So just be cool, Adrian—nothing's going to happen right away."

She went on into the living room, and Adrian, Jake, and Allie looked at each other. "Let's go outside," Adrian said, and without a word the others followed him out.

In the outside air Jake felt he could breathe again, felt he'd escaped an atmosphere that was thin on oxygen, stuffy, hard to breathe in and hard to see through clearly. Yet as soon as he stepped outside, he felt the weight of his father's treachery descend on him again. In Adrian's house, he'd briefly forgotten.

The sky was continually shifting, patchy clouds sliding across the sun and away again, draping them in shadow for a moment and then again in a hot glare. Without discussing where to go, they walked slowly toward Jake's house.

As they neared the house, ten or twelve noisy gulls swept overhead and descended on something in the weeds beside Roger's house. The three of them watched for a moment, in no hurry to move. Jake was glad for the distraction. He focused on their flutterings and raucous cries, on the way they elbowed each other to reach the food. Nothing on their tiny minds, as far as Jake could tell, but whatever edible substance lay in the weeds. The gull world was so perfectly simple.

They made sandwiches in Jake's kitchen. Allie took her plate to the couch and sat down to eat, but the boys wandered aimlessly with the food in their hands, looking out windows at nothing. Adrian left half his sandwich on the kitchen counter and paced the kitchen and living room with jerky steps.

Jake noticed that Allie was watching them both as if they were bombs about to go off.

Once he'd finished eating, Jake felt suddenly tired. He

didn't want to figure anything out; he just wanted things to be normal for a while.

He sat down beside Allie and pawed through magazines on the coffee table, finding nothing he wanted to look at, then reached under the table and took out his box of Magic cards.

"Why don't you guys play Magic?" Allie said unexpectedly.

For a second Jake remembered his father and Adrian playing chess while he sat on the sidelines. Allie didn't know the first thing about Magic. "You wouldn't mind?" he said to her.

"I don't care," she said. "I can just hang out and watch. You guys need to do something to calm down."

Adrian sank into the big armchair. "Okay, but I don't have my cards here."

"You can use mine."

"You gotta give me a decent deck, though. No crappy cards."

"Would I do that to you? Give you crappy cards?" Jake said with a look of mock outrage.

"Of course you would." Adrian was starting to seem more normal now, but there was still something nervous in his eyes, a faint crease in his forehead. Jake noticed this even while still feeling strange himself, almost numb, as though he needed more time to fully register all that had happened.

For now, though, he didn't want to think about any of it. Not about his father, not about the girlfriend, not about Adrian's pathetic father or his unpredictable stepsister. He just wanted to act like everything was okay.

He took out two decks and showed them to Adrian, and then they began making a new deck from the loose cards that nearly filled the box. As they talked about the cards, Adrian said suddenly, "Hey, don't we have to be quiet? Isn't your dad upstairs working?"

The words burst out of him as if long pent up. "You want to know where my dad is right now?" He told Adrian about the phone calls, about the bitter shock of discovering that his father was in a motel room with a girlfriend.

"Weird," Adrian said, then grimaced. "At least your father's smart, and he has a good job. And he hangs out with you some."

"Yeah, *some*," Jake muttered. But he thought of Adrian's father cowering in a corner, and knew he was lucky.

Adrian's thoughts, too, seemed to go to the far end of Tracktown. "That social worker that called—she could show up anytime, you know?" he said broodingly. "Or Miranda— it's like this sword hanging over my head. She picks up the phone, and then . . ."

Jake nodded. "Then some stupid social worker decides you ought to live in a foster home." He imagined Adrian deprived of the freedom he'd had for so long, stuck in a house with strangers, angry and miserable. Something like that actually could happen, Jake thought, even to Adrian, who'd always seemed so enviably free, unhindered by parents and their rules.

Adrian swallowed; he looked on the verge of tears. "It's

not just me, you know? It's my dad too. What'll they do about him? Maybe they'll put him in some institution. That's what he'd hate the most. He just wants to be left alone."

"I don't think they'd really do that," Allie said, but they all heard the hesitation in her voice. "Would they? I mean, he's not hurting anybody . . ."

Adrian stared at her with a flicker of hope, then dropped his eyes and said in a low voice, "I don't know."

He picked up some cards at random, fiddling with them, then looked up, meeting Jake's eyes. "So," he said slowly, "you're leaving tomorrow?"

"Yeah, for three nights. Then I'll be back for, I don't know, maybe four or five days before my mom takes me back to Wendell."

"Oh" was all Adrian said, but the brooding look deepened, and it occurred to Jake that Adrian was really going to miss him. It was true, after all, that Adrian had very few friends, not to mention the most messed-up family Jake had ever met.

"And then your dad will go back to his college?" Adrian asked.

"Yeah, right after my mom picks me up, I guess."

"God, I won't have anywhere to go," Adrian burst out, with a look of anguish on his face. "You and your dad—you're like—like a normal family—like I could come here sometimes and feel like a—a regular person with a real family." He looked down at the cards in his hands for a second, then threw them on the table as if they burned his fingers. He jumped up from the chair and began pacing the room, casting wild, angry glances at Jake.

"Now you're just gonna leave!" Adrian was almost shouting.

Taken aback, Jake stared at him. Of course he was leaving—he was a summer visitor in Tracktown; he was going back to his life in Wendell. How could Adrian be angry at him for that?

Allie stood up quickly. "Adrian, chill out," she pleaded. "It's not Jake's fault."

Jake found his voice, and it came out loud. "I'm still your friend."

Adrian faced them across the coffee table, visibly trembling. Then he spun on his heels and in two strides had seized the screen door handle. He yanked the door open so hard it banged against the wall, and then he was gone.

The bang echoed in Jake's mind, as he and Allie remained motionless for long seconds, too stunned to move. Then they rushed for the door.

Adrian was walking toward his house, walking so fast he appeared to be forcing himself not to run. Jake and Allie ran to catch up with him.

"Adrian," Allie said breathlessly as she reached his side. "Calm down. It's gonna be okay."

He didn't look at her, didn't answer. Jake, on the other side of Adrian, saw a hard tension in his face that abruptly reminded him of his expression at their football game in the park, before he attacked.

"Don't flip out," Jake said urgently. "You've gotta stay cool. We'll figure things out somehow."

Like Allie, he got no answer. Adrian went striding on, his face set in a straight-ahead stare. A muscle in his cheek twitched.

Only when they reached Adrian's house did he look at them, barely slowing his steps. "Just get out of here," he said roughly. "There's nothing you can do." Then, without another glance at them, he rushed up the steps and inside. The screen door slammed shut behind him. The main door must have received only a quick shove, because it swung more slowly, coming to rest with a small gap left open.

At the bottom of the steps, Jake and Allie looked anxiously at each other.

"Maybe we'd better back off," Jake said. "So he doesn't flip out on us."

"But—" Allie hesitated. "We can't just walk off and leave him like this."

Before Jake could answer, they heard Adrian shouting something they couldn't catch. Without a word Allie turned and ran up the steps. Jake took a deep breath and followed.

They burst into the house to find Miranda and Adrian arguing at the top of the stairs. Both of them glanced distractedly at the intruders and went on talking.

"Adrian, listen to me. I had to do something. He's gotten worse and worse, even in the last few days." Her voice dropped almost to a whisper. "An hour ago he was talking about killing himself."

"He'd never do that," Adrian said, but there was shock in his tone.

"You can't be sure," Miranda hissed back. "Nobody can."

"Who did you call?" Adrian demanded. "Those social services people?"

"No, I figured they'd take three weeks to do the paperwork before they'd even think about getting over here. I called my friend Marcia's mother. She's a psychiatric nurse, and I was hoping she'd come over and talk to him, but she has to be at the hospital all day. But she knows everybody in social services, and she got this social worker over there to promise to come and evaluate him."

"What do you mean, evaluate him?" Adrian said. Jake could see that his hand on the banister was white-knuckled, and his arm trembled slightly.

"Well, like, tell us if he should go to the hospital."

"Yeah? And what'll they do with me?" There was panic in his voice.

"They won't—"

"When?" Adrian demanded. "When are they coming?"

"Like, now. Like any minute."

"Now?" Adrian's voice went higher. He looked around desperately, as if some answer were to be found in the corners.

"Adrian, chill," Miranda said. "It's just this one woman. She's not coming with handcuffs to take you away."

"Yeah, well, this is how it starts," he said wildly. "This is—" He broke off, then suddenly dashed past Miranda into the nearest room, emerging seconds later with something in his hand. He shoved past his stepsister and ran down the stairs, almost knocking down Jake and Allie in his rush to the door.

They darted out behind him.

"What are you doing?" Jake shouted, and then he saw.

Adrian was down the steps and dashing for the white car, and the thing in his hand had to be the key he'd made weeks ago. Jake ran after him, hearing Allie and Miranda calling out behind him. In seconds Adrian was opening the door, sliding in under the wheel. The driver's side was nearer, and Jake ran straight toward it as the motor roared. "Adrian, wait, you gotta wait!"

"Go to hell, all of you!" He backed the car around, lurching, but then lost a few seconds trying to get into first, just enough time for Jake to seize the handle of the passenger door.

"Jake, don't!" Allie screamed, but he didn't answer.

"I'm coming with you," he panted as he threw himself into the front seat. "Adrian, you gotta slow down, don't—don't do crazy stuff," he gasped.

Miranda, or maybe Allie, was screaming something indistinct—Adrian was yelling at him, "Get out of here!"— and behind both voices he heard a weird rumbling he didn't have time to understand, like a distant earthquake, an under-current you could hear and feel, so deep it might have been his own racing blood.

Adrian understood it. He floored the gas, the car leaped forward, and Jake saw the train coming downhill toward Tracktown at a ferocious speed. "Adrian!" he screamed.

"I'm not getting trapped," Adrian screamed back, and aimed for the crossing. The car bumped onto the tracks with the train bearing down—Jake didn't know what he was scream-ing now—but they cleared it, they were free.

The train sped on, a gigantic, roaring, moving wall be-tween the white car and Tracktown.

20

They shot out onto the highway, and somewhere very close a horn blared and brakes squealed.

"God, Adrian," Jake yelled, groping for a seat belt. "You'll get us killed!"

The car swung to the left, up the long hill, instead of going right, toward town, the way Adrian had taken Jake before. They were flying into the countryside, past scattered houses and patches of woods, then barns and cornfields.

Adrian was trembling, and he was driving very fast. Jake, fastening the seat belt with clumsy hands, was trembling too, but he had to get through to Adrian somehow.

"Adrian," he said, trying to speak calmly, "slow down a little, okay? The main thing is not to get killed. That's the only thing that matters right now. Just slow down."

Adrian said nothing; he was tight-lipped and staring straight ahead. But he did ease off the gas slightly.

"Okay, that's it, that's what we need," Jake said soothingly. He sounded like his father, he realized suddenly. In a crisis his father could always calm everyone down. In a vivid flash he remembered a bad fall off his bike when he was eight, and the comfort of his father's hands and his father's words. What would Chris Berry say if he was in this car now? What would he do?

Adrian spoke before Jake could come up with an answer. "I knew I'd have to do this," he said shakily. "I planned it. Ever since Miranda came back, I thought if things got bad I'd just take the car and run."

"Run where?" Jake said.

"Anywhere I felt like." He paused, then added, "I even had a bag packed. But I forgot to get it."

Hot wind was loud through the open windows. They flashed past an antiques store in an old barn, a farmhouse with a sagging front porch, acres of tiny Christmas trees. Jake felt completely unmoored, traveling fast through strange territory, with no destination. But if *he* was lost, anchorless, what was Adrian?

"What were you going to do? I mean, where would you live? How would you get food?"

"Just—get a job. Wait tables, wash dishes or something. Sleep in a barn, maybe a bus station, I don't know." Adrian was trying to sound fearless about this grim prospect, Jake thought, but something in his voice gave him away.

They rounded a curve, then entered a long straight stretch with few trees and the largest fields they'd seen yet. The horizon, far down this gray road, looked miles away.

"So, for right now," Jake said hesitantly, "where are we going?"

Adrian flared up at once. "I don't know! How am I supposed to know?" He hit the steering wheel with a fist, swerving a little as he gave Jake an angry look. "I never planned on *you* being here anyway."

"Neither did I."

"Why did you get in the car?"

"To—to try to help."

"You can't," Adrian said shortly.

What kind of idiot am I? Jake thought, staring out at a sea of cornstalks heavy with ears. Adrian's right—I can't help him. There's nothing I can do. I have a home to go back to. I've got to go home.

But what was he going to say? "Take me back to Tracktown"? Adrian wasn't going to do that. If Adrian just let him out somewhere—someplace with a phone . . . He felt his pockets. He didn't even have quarters for a pay phone. He'd have to beg someone for the coins, and then call his dad in Ithaca. His dad, who would be totally furious.

And then what? How would he say good-bye to Adrian? "Good luck, pal—you're on your own"? "I'm leaving you out here in the middle of nowhere and going back to my dad"?

How could he ever do such a thing? Adrian had nobody.

But, as though Adrian had heard his thoughts, the car slowed a little, then slowed more, and the right-turn signal tinkled. A moment later they had glided to a stop in a convenience store's dusty parking area, empty except for one car.

They looked at each other.

"You better get out here," Adrian said shakily.

"I—" Jake felt his throat constrict. Wasn't there some way out, some way that he could go back to his life without abandoning Adrian?

He saw fear in Adrian's eyes, and he knew it took courage for Adrian to make this stop, to tell him to get out. But then something very different caught Jake's eye.

A man had stepped out the door of the convenience store, carrying a paper coffee cup with a plastic lid, and was walking toward their car. Before Jake could speak, the man became just a belt buckle and a big-bellied blue shirt filling the open window beyond Adrian, and then a bit of metal on the shirt that caught the sun as the man lowered his head and stared in.

In the same instant Adrian turned, saw the heavy-jawed face, pink with the day's heat, and made a startled twitch, then froze. A hand came up beside the face, palming a slim black case with an ID card, and a gruff voice said, "You got a driver's license?"

"Oh—oh, I'm not driving," Adrian said after a couple of weighty seconds. Jake could hear the smile in his voice, and wondered how Adrian could have managed to paste it on. "I'm just sitting here for a minute. My—my dad's driving. He just went to, you know, take a leak."

The face in the window was not smiling back. "I saw you drive in."

Nearly three hours later Jake sat, waiting, in a hard plastic chair before a desk in the tiny police station of the village of Blainesville. Behind the desk sat a woman named Officer Petty, but she wasn't paying the slightest attention to him, just filling out forms and typing on a computer.

They'd left the white car behind. The officer who'd brought them in had just gone off duty when he saw them—which explained why they hadn't spotted a patrol car—and had driven them to the station in his ancient Volvo sedan.

Officer Petty, after getting the story from the other officer, asked a lot of questions. Names, ages, addresses? Parents' names and phone numbers? Whose car? Why? Where were they going? And did Adrian know a car was a lethal weapon, a ton or more of steel that could have killed some innocent person—could have killed him and his young friend too, if he'd made a mistake, gone too fast, lost control, met up with a tree or a truck—the kind of thing teenage drivers did every day, even those who were old enough and had licenses and had taken driver's ed?

Officer Petty was plump, about the age of Jake's parents, with squinty eyes, brown hair pulled back in a careless pony-tail, and empty holes where her ears had been pierced. She didn't smile. Not once.

All the fight seemed to have drained out of Adrian. He answered in a scarcely audible voice and did not lie.

Jake too gave quiet, truthful answers. He was scared—scared of the sheer depth of trouble he was in, the likes of which he'd never gotten into before. Most of all, scared of his father's anger. But even with that cold, hard knot in his stomach that was all about himself, he knew that for Adrian the stakes were infinitely higher.

Officer Petty had called Miranda, and a friend had driven her to Blainesville to pick up Adrian and the car. There would be a referral to a probation officer, with whom Adrian would have to check in once a week, and possibly a visit from social services, Officer Petty had told Adrian and Miranda. Or maybe she'd come herself, and have a talk with Adrian's father. There would be no criminal charges as long as he followed the probation rules. No, they couldn't take Jake home too. He would be released only to a parent.

Adrian followed Miranda out the door in silence, shoulders slumped.

"Bye, Adrian," Jake said thickly.

"Bye," Adrian grunted, without looking at Jake.

Now Jake sat there in the station, alone except for Officer Petty. He stared at a calendar on the wall, at file cabinets, at the tall fan whirring in the corner, at an open window that showed him nothing except the one-truck fire station across the street. Officer Petty had left a message at Chris Berry's motel, and now they were waiting for him to call back.

A sense of unreality filled Jake's head. Was it possible that just this morning his father had left for Ithaca, Stephen had called to invite him on a trip, he'd called his father and discovered the girlfriend? And Adrian arguing with Miranda, then growing more and more upset as he realized that Jake and his father would soon be leaving? The rush to Adrian's house, the news that sent him over the edge? The dash to the car, close call with the train, the wild drive whose unplanned destination had turned out to be the lone police station in this tiny village he'd never heard of?

How could all that happen in one day? How could he still be the same Jake after all of that?

And now the sun had dropped just low enough to glare through the west-facing window, in a white shaft of light that bleached the posters tacked on the wall, posters about CPR and the Heimlich maneuver and first aid. The afternoon seemed a year long, and still his father did not call.

Occasionally the phone did ring, and Jake stiffened, listening hard, as Officer Petty spoke briskly into it, but in seconds it was apparent that the person on the other end was not Jake's father. And once Officer Petty dialed it herself and spoke in a totally different voice, a voice Jake couldn't have imagined coming out of her, the sweet voice of a mother speaking to a child.

At one point she disappeared into the back of the station for a few minutes. He heard a toilet flush, and when she came back, she looked at him for the first time in an hour. "Bathroom's back there if you need it."

"Okay." He didn't move.

She stepped behind her desk again, opened a tiny refrigerator next to the file cabinets, and pulled out a can of root beer. She held it out to him without a word, and he took it gratefully. After a couple of sips he remembered to say "thanks." Meanwhile she'd rummaged around and pulled out a few old magazines, which she placed on the chair next to his before going back to her paperwork.

His father must be in the library, working through the long afternoon. Or out somewhere with the girlfriend.

He read a couple of articles in an old *Sports Illustrated*, without taking in very much. It helped pass the time, but reading about spring training on a hot August day just added to the feeling of unreality. He put down the *SI* and paged slowly through *Bass Fisherman* and *American Sportsman*.

He kept imagining his father coming back to the motel and the desk clerk handing him a piece of paper, which his father would puzzle over, shaking his head. Blainesville police? Why would they be calling him? Chris Berry had probably never even heard of Blainesville, any more than Jake had, until today. But then he'd be alarmed, he'd think it must have something to do with his son. He'd call right away, and then he'd rush to his car and drive to Blainesville.

He'd have to leave his girlfriend in Ithaca, leave his research unfinished, because Jake had gotten in trouble. He'd be incredibly angry. He'd ask himself why he'd ever offered to spend the summer with Jake, and he'd be glad that at least he'd soon get rid of him, turn him over to his mother again.

Jake felt tears well up, and he blinked them back angrily and stared at the magazine in his lap.

Damn it, why didn't his father just call and get this over with? How much longer could he stand this waiting, this awful boredom with something he so much dreaded at the end of it? He threw the magazine down on the other chair and put his face in his hands.

What if his father went straight from the library to dinner, a long, leisurely restaurant dinner with the girlfriend? What if somehow he didn't get the message till tomorrow? Would Jake be locked in a cell all night? He was twelve years old—things like this weren't supposed to happen to a kid.

Adrian was just thirteen.

Chris Berry finally called around 5:30. Officer Petty told him what had happened, then held out the phone to Jake. Slowly he got up and walked to the desk to take it. "Hello," he said quietly.

"Are you all right?"

"Yeah, I guess."

"Well, if you are, it's a miracle," his father snapped, adding incredulously, "You got in a car with *Adrian* driving? What the hell were you thinking?"

"I—I can't explain right now." Jake swallowed hard. "Can you just come and pick me up?"

He heard a long, slow exhale on the other end. "I don't

have much choice, do I? Okay, we'll talk when I get there. Give the phone back to the officer so I can get directions."

More waiting. Officer Petty told Jake that Blainesville was closer to Ithaca than Tracktown was, and his dad should arrive in about an hour.

Jake nodded bleakly.

"I'm about to call the deli. What kind of sub do you want?" she asked.

"Oh," he said numbly. "I'm—not too hungry."

She frowned at him. "You can't face your father on an empty stomach," she said severely. "Ham and Swiss? Turkey? Meatball?"

Jake felt utterly empty, but he didn't know whether that was the same as being hungry. "I don't have any money," he told her.

"You don't need it. We don't starve kids around here. Now what do you want?"

When the food came, fifteen minutes later, Jake was glad he'd accepted. He didn't quite finish the turkey-and-Swiss sub, but he felt stronger and less hollow after eating. He walked around a little, looking at the posters on the walls or gazing out the window at the fire station. He tried not to watch the clock.

A car door slammed outside the station, and Jake went nervously to the window, but the car wasn't his father's, and the man who'd emerged from it was walking away down the street.

The next time he heard a car door, he saw his father striding quickly toward the station, frowning. Jake's hands clenched in his pockets. A second later his father was inside. He said a curt hello to his son, talked briefly with Officer Petty, and a moment later he and Jake were sitting in the station wagon.

Chris Berry made no move to start the car. Jake stared straight ahead through the dusty windshield, but he had a feeling his father was looking at him. The silence lengthened.

"I suppose you know," his father began at last, in a tone of controlled anger, "what a stupid thing that was to do. Going for a joyride with a kid who's nowhere near old enough to drive. You could have been killed, and so could he. I always thought you had more sense than that."

Jake kept looking straight ahead.

"I suppose you also know," his father continued, voice rising, "what a pain in the butt this whole episode is for me. I leave for just one single day, to do some research and see a friend, and you go get yourself in trouble with the police—so I have to interrupt everything I'm trying to do just to drive out here in the middle of nowhere and pick you up."

Jake could feel his breath coming harder, pain and anger rising in him.

His father slammed a fist on the steering wheel. "You're twelve years old, for God's sake. A reasonable person would think you could be left alone for a few hours without getting in trouble. But maybe you just *wanted* to cause some trouble. What about it, Jake? Were you so upset about Angela that you just had to find a way to ruin my trip?"

So much fear was inside Jake—the old fear that if he caused trouble, his father wouldn't want him around, wouldn't want to come home to Jake and Lena. Some trace of that fear had been in him all summer. There was guilt too—he *had* ruined his father's trip. But anger surged at the injustice of his father's words, at all the ways his father failed to understand what had really happened. And for once, Jake's anger overrode the fear and guilt.

"I wasn't trying to ruin your trip!" he yelled, turning to face his father. "I got in the car to try to help Adrian. It wasn't some stupid joyride. You don't know how bad things are for him, you don't know what's going on at his house." He took a heaving breath. "And anyway I'm your *son*! All summer you've been acting like your work's the most important thing in the world—" He gasped, fighting back tears. "All my *life* you've been acting like that. Like I'm just something you'll put up with now and then, when you're not busy working."

"That's crap," his father said angrily. "Grow up a little. I have to work, I'm not on vacation all summer."

But Jake wasn't going to stop. Tears were flowing now, and he slapped angrily at his eyes and cheeks, hating the tears. They humiliated him, but that only made him angrier.

"You left me!" he yelled. "You left me and Mom in Wendell like you just didn't want us anymore. And you went five hundred miles away and you had a whole new life, and you kept me out."

Jake could see through the blur that his father's eyes were riveted on his face, that his father opened his mouth to speak again, then shut it. Jake could scarcely believe he was saying all this, as though the words that burst out of him were an act of desperation, like Adrian's wild dash to the car, across the train tracks, out to the endless, unknown highway.

He kept going. "You never told me you had a girlfriend. You've never let me visit you. I've never even seen where you live. You don't even want me in your life."

Now his father sounded more stunned than angry. "That's not true, Jake—you know that."

"You want me way off in Wendell," Jake whispered. His vision cleared, and his eyes were burning into his father's. "You want to put me on a shelf and take me down when you feel like it. Not when *I* feel like it. Not when I need you."

The words hovered between them. Chris Berry shook his head, started to speak, and again stopped. He had the look of someone struggling with a decision, struggling with himself.

Then he took a deep breath and finally spoke, his voice as quiet as his son's. "I didn't know you felt like that." He pulled Jake's shoulders toward him and held him awkwardly across the hand brake. "I'm sorry, Jake. I'm so sorry."

Jake felt his father's collarbone under his cheek, and smelled soap and sweat in the blue cotton shirt. He pressed his whole face into that shirt and tried to stop the tears from seeping.

21

Five days later Jake sat on Adrian's front steps, taking a breather from shooting and dribbling. On the step below him, Maddy was playing with two small dolls, using Adrian's cigarettes, which he'd left on the top step, to mark the outline of a house for them. A breeze kept lifting her wispy blond hair. The weather had turned cooler, and for once the late-morning sun felt pleasant rather than burning hot.

"Like this," Adrian said, showing Allie his form in a set shot. "You try it." Ever since she and Maddy had wandered down the street an hour or so earlier, he had been telling her she had to learn basketball.

"You're tall," he'd said. "You've got good hands."

Allie had kept shaking her head. "I've never been good at sports. Any sport," she'd added with a nervous little laugh.

But she'd finally agreed to try.

Watching, Jake felt a twinge of jealousy, but at the same time he was glad Adrian would have Allie—someone calm and caring and smart—to hang around with. Because this was Jake's last day in Tracktown.

The days since he'd jumped into the car with Adrian had gone unbelievably fast. On the drive from Blainesville to Tracktown, as the daylight dimmed, Jake had explained why he'd done what he'd done, telling his father everything he knew about Adrian and his family. It wasn't that he'd forgotten his promise to Adrian. But the promise seemed to belong to another era, to a time before that dash across the tracks, when the train had divided them from Tracktown. And after all, his father wasn't going to do anything to get Adrian taken away. What mattered now was for Jake and his father to understand each other.

When they turned off the highway into Tracktown, there was no one to be seen outside Adrian's house, only the usual clutter of junk and weeds.

Jake and his father had sat on the dock that night in the darkness, listening to the lake water slapping against boats and docks, and they'd talked about how the summer had gone, and about their old life with Mom.

"Why didn't you finish your PhD back when you started it?" Jake asked. "Why did you wait till I was in fourth grade to work on it again?"

"Money," his father said. "That's the short answer. Your mother and I had this beautiful baby boy, and she didn't want to go back to work right away. And I had loans from my undergraduate days to pay off. It just seemed like I'd better earn some money first."

"Was that—okay with you?"

"Not really," his father said quietly. "It was a big disappointment, but it was just something that had to be done. And then a few years later, when I thought about going back to finish the degree, I'd lost my momentum. I knew I'd forgotten so much of what I'd learned earlier." He looked out toward the far shore, with its sprinkles of lights. "I was afraid if I tried again, I'd fail."

"But you did it," Jake said.

"Yes." His father hesitated, choosing his words. "The only way—I thought—to be sure I wouldn't fail was to make the PhD program my absolute top priority, all the time." He put a hand on Jake's knee. "I guess I didn't realize how hard that would be for you."

Remembering those days, Jake felt some of the old resentment, but it seemed less poisonous now that they were talking and listening to each other.

"But then you left," Jake said. "You got the degree and got this job and moved."

His father shook his head. "I don't expect you to understand this, Jake. But . . ." Again he seemed to search for words. "Your mother and I hadn't been really happy together in a long time. It wasn't her fault—she's a good person. It wasn't anyone's fault. But once I knew the degree was becoming a reality, and the kind of job I'd always wanted was within my reach, and I'd be moving to a new town, I realized—well, I realized I needed to go there alone. I needed a new life."

"So you just left us behind," Jake said, the old bitterness rising.

"That's not fair," his father protested. "I visited, I talked to you on the phone."

Jake shrugged. "Yeah, a little."

They sat in silence for a few minutes. Then Jake said, "Why didn't you ever let me visit you?"

His father shrugged uncomfortably. "Didn't seem like a good idea, to put you on a plane by yourself. Expensive too."

"Yeah, but what was the *real* reason?" Jake said sharply.

"What do you mean?" his father's voice rose indignantly.

"I just don't think that's the whole reason. I think it's— your girlfriend. Maybe you didn't want her to know you have a kid."

"She's *always* known about you, Jake. I showed her pictures. I told her about you playing baseball."

"Okay, then why couldn't I come and stay for a few days? I asked and asked and you always said no."

Chris Berry looked at him hard. "All right, Jake. I'm going to tell you something, and you're going to have to try to be grown up enough to understand it. And it's something you can't tell your mother. I'll tell her myself, sometime soon, but I've put it off because I don't want to hurt her any more than I already have."

"Okay," Jake said slowly.

His father took a deep breath. "I moved in with Angela just three months after I started the job. *Ridiculously* fast. I'm sure a lot of people thought we were both crazy. But what they don't know is that I'd known Angela before. We were friends in college, but she had boyfriends—not me—and after graduation we lost touch.

"When I took the job I had no idea she was teaching there. I'd gone there to start over, to have a life with no entanglements. But once I'd spent a little time with her, I realized we still knew each other, deep down, and I realized it wasn't 'no entanglements' I wanted, it was the *right* entanglement. I moved into her house, and we've been very happy."

Jake thought this over for a moment. "Then why did you decide to come to Tracktown for the summer?"

"Angela had to be in Europe for most of June and July, doing research—her field is eighteenth-century France. I could have tagged along, but it would have been expensive, and impossible for me to get my own work done. Besides," he added, smiling, "I wanted to spend some time with my son."

Jake nodded without returning the smile. "But it still seemed like you were always working."

His father sighed. "I'll never be the perfect father, Jake. And my work *is* important to me, and I needed to get a lot of it done. But even if everything wasn't perfect, I'm still really glad I could spend this summer with you."

"Yeah," Jake said, sliding his feet off the edge of the dock and into the cool water, the not-so-clean but beautiful, living lake. "Me too."

The plans with Stephen, Chris Berry said, had to be changed. He didn't think Jake should rush off at noon the day after so much had happened. So Chris had called Stephen's father and gotten directions, promising to drive Jake to Stephen's grandmother's house the following day. He could still spend two nights there before being brought back to Tracktown.

So Jake had spent a quiet Sunday in Tracktown. Though he'd protested his father's plan at first, he found that he was tired, and it was good to just hang around for a while. Adrian showed up around 10:00 A.M., dragging himself into the house as if his sneakers were full of lead, and this time Chris didn't go upstairs to work. He sat with the boys in the kitchen while they ate cereal, and he asked Adrian what was happening at home.

"Sorry, Adrian," Jake put in quickly. "I had to tell him—I mean, I had to explain, like, why I was out in the car with you in Blainesville."

" 'S okay," Adrian said. His voice was dull and lifeless.

He had to see a probation officer once a week, starting Tuesday. That wouldn't be too bad, from what he'd heard. But so much else was uncertain.

The social worker had arrived soon after Adrian and Jake had fled, and she had talked with Miranda and Malcolm. She was going to make an appointment for Malcolm at the county mental health offices so that he could be evaluated further. Would Malcolm actually go? And if he did—or even if he didn't—who could say what that might lead to?

Meanwhile, Miranda had both car keys, and she wore them on a necklace twenty-four hours a day.

"I don't want to get sent away," Adrian said. There was a haunted look in his eyes. "But my dad's not getting any better."

That night Jake's father insisted that he call his mother and tell her what had happened—tell her about Adrian, the car, the police, everything.

"She'll freak out, Dad," Jake protested.

"No, she won't. And I'm certainly not going to conceal something this important from your mother, no matter how she might react. So pick up the phone. I'll be right here listening to make sure she gets the whole story." He sat down on the couch, arms folded, and watched as Jake reluctantly dialed home.

Lena Berry wanted a lot of explanations. And then she wanted Jake to do some listening. "Let me get this straight," she said. "You wanted to stop your friend from doing something crazy—which he was already doing—so you jumped in the front seat of a car driven by a thirteen-year-old kid who was terribly upset. Am I right so far?"

"More or less," Jake muttered.

"Did this just happen to be a driver training car, with an extra steering wheel and a brake on the right side? So you could take over if the driver got a little out of control?"

"Oh Mom." Jake rolled his eyes.

"Then there was nothing you could do by getting in that car except get yourself killed. Have some *sense*, Jake."

She went on this way for some time before Jake could change the subject and let her know about the visit with Stephen.

The next day Jake's father drove him to Stephen's grandmother's house, a cottage beside a much smaller lake less than an hour away. It was mid-morning when they arrived, just in time for Stephen's father's famous French toast. Jake had two glorious days with Stephen and his family—swimming, kayaking, card games, squirt-gun fights, barbecues—before they drove him back to Tracktown.

Sometimes, during the quieter parts of those two days, Jake thought about his father and all the things they'd said to each other. The feeling inside him was warmer, more solid and satisfied, than the way he'd felt about his father for a long time.

He thought about Adrian too, one morning when he woke up early in the little cottage bedroom, with its pink-flowered curtains and the old-fashioned bedspreads with tufts of cotton like rows of tiny cabbages, and Stephen snoring in the other twin bed. He felt a little guilty, having fun here while Adrian was back in Tracktown, in trouble and worried about the future. Jake thought of that mad dash for the car and out of Tracktown, and hoped Adrian wouldn't do anything that crazy again. Jake remembered Adrian jumping him, pushing him deep into the lake, out of nowhere. He remembered the football game when Adrian had turned on him, again out of nowhere.

But it wasn't exactly nowhere, Jake thought. It was out of this crazy mess Adrian lived in, all this uncertainty and anger and fear. No father or mother he could look up to or count on. Maybe, Jake thought, surprising himself, Adrian had a little too much freedom.

Then Stephen rolled over and opened one eye at him. With a twist of his head, Jake roared like the MGM lion in the old movies. Stephen roared sleepily back, and the day began.

Stephen's family dropped Jake off around eleven and drove away, all of them waving.

"I was in the middle of making coffee," his father said. "Come on in the kitchen and talk to me."

Jake told him about his stay with Stephen, bouncing around the kitchen as he talked, tapping out a flurry of rhythms on the cabinets in between questions and answers.

Then his father said, "Want to hear some good news about Adrian?"

"Sure," Jake said immediately, halting in mid-rhythm.

"I've talked to him a few times while you were away. Miranda took his father to the appointment at the mental health office, and the doctor prescribed some medication to make him less anxious. He's going to have regular appointments with the doctor and a therapist. And the social worker doesn't see any need for Adrian to be sent to a foster home."

"That's great," Jake said, relief flooding through him. "That's so great."

"*But*—" his father went on, "he'd better not put a toe out of line. He has to see the probation officer every week, and go to school and behave himself."

"Sure," Jake nodded.

"There's something else I want to tell you." His father went over to the booth and sat down with his coffee mug, beckoning to Jake to join him. "Or"—he hesitated—"something I want to *ask* you."

"What?" said Jake, sliding onto the bench.

"Would you like—well, how would you feel about going to my house—to visit for a couple of days?"

Jake stared at him. "You'd—you'd let me come?"

"It might not be easy," his father warned. "You'd meet Angela. And she has two daughters, younger than you, who might be there—they're coming back any day now from a vacation with their dad. You'd be meeting this whole other family."

"Daughters?" Jake said wonderingly. His father hadn't mentioned them before. That would be weird. He hoped they'd still be on vacation. And this woman, Angela, who'd taken his mother's place . . . would he like her? How *could* he like her? It all sounded very confusing.

"I'd like for you to come, Jake. I want Angela to meet you. And I'd like for you to know about the way I live now."

Jake took a deep breath. "Yeah," he said. "Yeah, I'd like to come."

"Good." His father's smile made those crinkles around his eyes. "I already called your mother, and she said okay. She'll pick you up at the Syracuse airport on Sunday. And now you'd better pack, because we're leaving first thing tomorrow."

He'd packed in a flash, then hurried down the street. That was when he'd found Adrian out front, shooting baskets.

"Good news, man," he called as he walked up. Adrian grinned at him without a word. Jake snatched the ball out of his hands and took a shot that bounced off the rim.

"Pathetic, Berry," Adrian said, and they launched into a hard, fast game of one-on-one. Then Allie and Maddy had arrived, and Adrian's attention was all for Allie.

When he grew tired of watching Adrian give Allie basketball lessons, Jake said, "Guess what, guys?"

"What?" Allie said, handing the ball back to Adrian, who did a perfect layup.

"I'm leaving tomorrow."

"You are?" Adrian paused with the ball in his hands. "I thought you had a few more days."

"My dad is taking me to see where he lives. Then I'm going to fly home after a couple of days."

"Oh no, you can't leave so soon," Allie said, looking upset.

"We'll miss you." Then she smiled. "I guess we'll just have to have a humongous good-bye party."

"Party! Party!" Maddy shouted.

They had pizza at Jake's house that night, even Maddy, though she wasn't allowed to stay long. Peter came too, and brought Jake a trilobite as a going-away present. Allie had made a chocolate cake with BYE, JAKE! written in green icing, and they ate fat slices of it while listening to Chris Berry's old rock 'n' roll songs.

The Beach Boys were crooning "California Girls" when the evening train roared through. My next-to-last Tracktown train, Jake thought, the couch vibrating under him. He watched through the window as rust-red boxcars clattered and squealed past the house.

Peter had to go home at nine, and Jake went to the door with him to say good-bye.

"I'll e-mail you sometime," Peter said earnestly. "I'll tell you what else I've found."

"Cool," Jake said, grinning, and Peter took off running down the street in the deepening dusk.

At ten o'clock Jake's father said they had to get to bed, and that he and Jake could walk the other two home.

"Allie's house is too far," Jake whined, earning a whack from Adrian that rippled through his hair without touching his head.

They stepped out into the warm night, full of cicada and cricket sounds in between the passing of cars on the highway. The nearer of Tracktown's two streetlights cast a dim circle on the street and the gleaming tracks.

At Allie's door they said good night, and Allie said, "Have a safe trip." Then she reached for Jake and hugged him tightly, startling him, leaving him stiff but pleased.

"I'll see you around, Adrian," she said, opening her door.

"Yeah, I'll see you."

When the door closed behind her, the three of them walked on, into the dark patch between streetlights. Adrian took out his cigarettes and a book of matches.

"I didn't know you smoked," Chris Berry said with a surprised frown.

"Sometimes," Adrian answered casually. The match flared, for an instant spotlighting his face.

"I don't suppose there's any need to tell you how stupid that is."

"Nope." Adrian blew out a long puff of smoke. Jake's father just shook his head.

"Hey," Jake said, remembering something. "Did you ever find out who called that social worker and told her to call you guys?"

"Naah, she wouldn't say," Adrian replied. "But I think I know. I'd bet anything it was Peter's grandpa. He's watching all the time, you know? Watching everybody in Tracktown."

They were approaching Peter's house, which was dark except for one upstairs window. Jake looked at the porch, at the old man's empty chair. "I bet you're right," he murmured.

At the bottom of Adrian's steps they stopped and looked at each other in the dim aura of the streetlight.

"Take care of yourself, Adrian," Chris Berry said, his voice firm and serious. "You haven't got an easy situation. But you're smart. Just stay in school and stay out of trouble, and you'll be all right."

"Yeah," Adrian said. In the dusky light it was hard to be sure, but Jake thought he swallowed hard before speaking again, and his hand with the cigarette shook a little. "Listen, thanks—thanks for everything."

Beyond him, where the light circle ended and the street ended, Jake saw a figure standing near the tracks, a man with a scarf around his neck. Jake shivered. "There's Jonah," he said softly.

Adrian didn't turn to look. "I know, I already saw him." He dropped the cigarette and stepped on it.

They all said their good-byes then, and Jake and his father watched Adrian walk up the steps. When he opened the door, light streamed out, and for a second Adrian's lean silhouette appeared, then vanished as the door closed behind him.

For a moment Jake and his father stood looking up at the quiet house. Light shone through curtains in the two upstairs windows; a downstairs light winked off. Jake glanced again toward the end of the street, but Jonah had disappeared.

They turned and walked back toward Sam Weesner's house, toward sleep and one more rude awakening, toward whatever the next day's journey could bring.